S0-BZU-538

"I want to sleep with you," Bridget murmured

Words were forming before Dermott thought them through. If the truth be told, he'd waited just as many years to speak them as he'd waited to have her beneath him in bed. "You're not going to play with my emotions, Bridge. Not now. Not at this stage of the game."

She looked crushed, her face falling. "Game?" she managed to say. "It's just sex...."

He couldn't believe how hot she looked for it, either, as she offered the half lift of a bare shoulder that seemed so silky, smooth and delicious that his mouth watered. "Aren't you even curious?" she asked.

That was the problem. He had been for years. He'd dropped plenty of hints about them winding up between the sheets. Now he tried to look unaffected, even though he was painfully aroused. "You're the one who always said no."

"That was then."

He leaned closer. Her breath was on his cheek, his lips and in his hair. "And this is now?"

Nodding, she whispered, "Just sex."

But they both knew it was more than that.

Dear Reader,

Manhattan aside, the American rural South is my favorite place to write about. No one can ignore the pull of the environment—the slow, sexy drawls of Southern men, the mysterious woods thick with ancient, moss-hung cypress trees, the ambling quality of life, not to mention the lure of so much living history.

So welcome to the second installment of BIG APPLE BRIDES! I hope you'll have a blast with middle sister Bridget Benning as she joins her buddy Dermott and flies off to battle ghosts on a plantation, determined to end the wedding curse holding her back!

In May 2005 watch for *I Thee Bed...*, the last book in the BIG APPLE BRIDES miniseries.

Writing romance for the past decade has been a great delight of my life, as has reading so many upbeat love stories designed to lift our spirits, feed our souls, make us laugh and nurture our faith in the lighter side of life—love!

Happy reading!

Jule McBride

JULE McBRIDE

NIGHTS IN WHITE SATIN

HARLEQUIN®

TORONTO • NEW YORK • LONDON
AMSTERDAM • PARIS • SYDNEY • HAMBURG
STOCKHOLM • ATHENS • TOKYO • MILAN • MADRID
PRAGUE • WARSAW • BUDAPEST • AUCKLAND

If you purchased this book without a cover you should be aware that this book is stolen property. It was reported as "unsold and destroyed" to the publisher, and neither the author nor the publisher has received any payment for this "stripped book."

ISBN 0-373-69213-7

NIGHTS IN WHITE SATIN

Copyright © 2005 by Julianne Moore.

All rights reserved. Except for use in any review, the reproduction or utilization of this work in whole or in part in any form by any electronic, mechanical or other means, now known or hereafter invented, including xerography, photocopying and recording, or in any information storage or retrieval system, is forbidden without the written permission of the publisher, Harlequin Enterprises Limited, 225 Duncan Mill Road, Don Mills, Ontario, Canada M3B 3K9.

All characters in this book have no existence outside the imagination of the author and have no relation whatsoever to anyone bearing the same name or names. They are not even distantly inspired by any individual known or unknown to the author, and all incidents are pure invention.

This edition published by arrangement with Harlequin Books S.A.

® and TM are trademarks of the publisher. Trademarks indicated with ® are registered in the United States Patent and Trademark Office, the Canadian Trade Marks Office and in other countries.

www.eHarlequin.com

Printed in U.S.A.

Prologue

Big Swamp, Florida,
a dark stormy February night in the late 1860s...

"Hurry, Miss Marissa! We must run!"

"Don't you tell me what to do, Lavinia," returned Miss Marissa Jennings in a hushed, terrified drawl as thick as cold molasses. She cast the Creole housekeeper a furious look, her green eyes glistening with tears, then she glanced around the parlor of her fiancé's plantation, her pale fingers clutching the skirt of the wedding dress she'd waited so long to wear, her mind barely able to process that she might not marry Forrest tonight as planned. Surely, he and Reverend George were on their way, she thought, her fingers tightening around the gown's white satin. Lifting the hem above her ankles, she exposed a pair of white slippers, preparing to do as Lavinia had said—run! The gorgeous cluster of diamonds Forrest had given her sparkled when she glanced down. It seemed centuries ago that she'd been given the ring, centuries since her slippers had been hand-beaded by her mama, long before the war drew near and they'd all blissfully envisioned the Jenningses and Hartleys gathering at Hartley House for the wedding.

"Hurry!" Lavinia urged as lightning flashed, her voice scarcely audible over cannonballs, rifle fire and the shouts of looting Yankees as they circled nearer, some on foot, some whipping neighing horses into a frenzy. "We've got to hide in the swamp!"

"We can't go out there, Lavinia!" The gale-force wind would sweep them from their feet, killing them before any Yankees could. "What if Forrest comes?"

"He'll find us."

Another lie. A deafening boom sounded, and a flash of fire lit the sky in bright white light that threw the parlor into bas relief. For a second, Marissa could see Lavinia clearly—a small-boned woman who wore her hair plaited in tidy rows—before they were plunged into near-darkness again. Only a lit taper in the housekeeper's hand illuminated the fear in her eyes, the flickering, wind-tossed flame tinting her skin with a red glow like that which burned beyond the windows.

Marissa's eyes blurred with tears, her heart beating in terror for her groom. Surely he was on his way! She'd sooner die than leave this home they were to share! How could she abandon things her beloved Forrest had worked so hard to attain? How could she let all this beauty be pawed by crass, looting Yankees?

"We should have gone weeks ago, Miss Marissa!" assured Lavinia, pushing Marissa toward a doorway. Tears splashed Marissa's cheeks, falling as hard as the rain against the windowpanes as she cast a last glance around the parlor—taking in a chandelier Forrest had brought from Paris, then a pedestal table and a fireplace hewn from unpolished jagged pieces of local quarry rock. Forrest had been so precise when decorating the room, especially regarding how she should pose for her portrait and where it should hang, the key to their secret hiding place. The portrait had been removed now, but she could still see marks indicating its position.

"The chandelier!" she protested, her heart wrenching. Forrest had called it their mistletoe. Oh, how they'd kissed beneath it, holding each other and shuddering with need, wanting to consummate their passion, but reined in by the desperation of restraint, knowing it would be well worth the wait. She and Lavinia had tugged on the heavy light fixture, hoping to hide it, although it wouldn't fit beneath the upstairs floorboards where they'd put the jewelry—all but the ring still on Marissa's finger. The chandelier seemed to have grown a mind of its own, though, as if it had decided it wasn't leaving Hartley House; it had taken root in a medallion of ceiling molding, as immobile as cypress trees and salt marshes.

Her heart aching, Marissa sucked in a sharp breath. She and Lavinia had been hiding here, cut off from civilization for what felt like eternity, the field hands long gone, and now Marissa realized she'd been a fool, waiting for Forrest to come back from the war. And yet he'd returned. Just a week ago, she'd seen him for the first time in two years. Appearing like a vision from one of Lavinia's prophetic dreams, he'd been far off, coming down the shell-covered driveway in the heat of a Florida February afternoon.

It was long after the morning dew had burned off and the sun had risen high in the sky, looking wave-like as it shimmered on the driveway. Forrest had appeared, without warning, wounded but still walking, using his rifle as a crutch.

Marissa had fainted dead away, but Lavinia had run for the salts, and Marissa had awakened to find her own true love peppering her cheeks with kisses. Of course, Forrest had wanted to turn around and head for the war again, but he'd suffered a gunshot wound and his leg needed tending. Even worse, he'd said the Yankees were coming.

Oh, she'd wanted nothing more than to nurse her well-loved warrior. As he'd rested this week, she'd sat beside him, staring at the man she intended to wake beside every day of her life and whose babies would soon be growing inside her. They'd decided to marry before his return to the front and spend at least one passionate night. And then she and Lavinia would travel to Marissa's sister's house two counties away. It never occurred to them that the Yankees would get this far, nearly to the front door of Hartley House. Come tomorrow, Forrest was to have joined the few men left in town to march north. But Forrest was dead. He had to be. No one could survive what was happening now.

"Follow me," Lavinia commanded, turning on her heel and heading through the parlor, toward a back door.

Marissa had frozen in place. Forrest's ring! She couldn't wear it into the swamp. Now she wished she'd let Lavinia hide it under the floorboards with the rest of the jewelry. There wasn't time to go back upstairs, though. Her eyes darted around the parlor—taking in the pedestal table, the space where her portrait had hung and the mantle. She'd hide the ring in her and Forrest's special place, she thought, her heart pounding when she knelt, her heavy white skirts cushioning her knees as she twisted the ring from her finger. *Oh, please, be safe here,* she thought, slipping the ring into the hiding place. Then she wrenched as Lavinia's voice sounded again. "Hurry!"

She ran then, nearly tripping on the hem of the dress, her heart lurching as she reached the back door. Howling wind caught the edge of the door, nearly tearing it from its hinges. Her finger felt bare now, bereft of the symbol of Forrest's love, but there was no time to think about it because the door slammed against the house, and Lavinia's taper flickered out.

Thunderclouds raced across the moon as Lavinia pocketed the candle and whispered, "This night's the devil's handiwork, missy."

Shuddering, Marissa took in the shadowy shapes riding like phantom demons across the sky. There were skulls and crossbones. Angry steeds. Lavinia wasn't lying. She dealt in herbs and voodoo and was known to have premonitions. Marissa grasped her hand and stepped onto the lawn, her head bent against the onslaught of wind and rain. The temperature had dropped, the heat of the day giving way to cooling northern winds blowing in from the sea. It was hard to run in the gown, but Marissa dodged trees in the yard, the soupy mud sucking at her slippers. Stumbling, she could barely make out the ancient moss-hung cypress trees at the edge of the swamp.

Something snagged her dress and a cry tore from her throat as satin ripped away. Her sisters—all accomplished seamstresses—had insisted on making the gown, and now it was going to be ruined. They'd made so many plans that seemed silly now, never imagining war could touch their lives.

A jagged finger of lightning illuminated the swamp, and Marissa saw Lavinia once more, a tiny firecracker of a woman with skin the shiny red color of glazed clay pottery. Beyond was the Benchley plantation, not that the Benchleys had offered assistance, even though their land was on higher, dryer ground. Men were on the shell road now, and soon they'd be in the house. Once there, they'd see remnants of dinner, and know people were hiding somewhere. Armoires would disclose the inhabitants had been women and, soon, hungry men would be in the yard, hunting for her and Lavinia.

"Get in the water, Miss Marissa!"

"Grab these roots, Lavinia," Marissa returned as a torch flared, the fingers of pale, delicate hands gripping the mangled claws of cypress roots, just as a gust lifted her skirt and her feet, which almost left the ground. Lavinia snatch the skirt, to steady them both, right before Marissa plunged into the pulsing swirl of black waters. Madness, she thought as Lavinia followed into the icy water. Another torch flared, then Marissa heard a male voice from far off, the words unclear, but gruff, making her swoon because she'd heard what vagabond soldiers did to women. Downwind, the waters fed salt marshes, then tidewaters that met the Atlantic, and now, as she sank into the pull of currents, spiders seemed to climb the ladder of her spine; her body shook as she imagined gators circling beneath her, and she wished her gown wasn't ballooning and deflating as the white skirts became soaked.

"Who's out there?" came a Yankee shout, traveling on the wind. "I saw you run! Show yourselves!"

Lavinia grasped Marissa's shoulder in assurance, but when the sky lit up again, men on horses fanned across the yard…men whose faces were no longer shadows, but rather, clearly defined, made hard by a war in which they'd seen too much killing.

The heavy winds whipped up, lifting twigs and sending them spinning, and suddenly, the hand on her shoulder was gone—simply gone! Marissa's own hand was almost ripped from the cypress root. She gasped, and when lightning cracked again, she realized the other woman really was gone! *Lavinia!* Had she really lost her hold, been swept away? Was that her head bobbing in the water? A hand waving? Or just tricks of Marissa's imagination? Marissa wrenched once more, and in another lightning flash saw…Forrest?

She felt faint. Her wet corset clung to her ribs, stealing her breath. Surely, it was her imagination, but now she saw Forrest running along the shell drive, coming toward the Yankees in the yard. Had he lost his mind? No…like her, he was in love. He was searching for her, but if she called out, they'd both be killed.

Yankees were in the house now. A taper flared in a window. Oh, how she hated those men who were defiling the home of her beloved, where she was meant to experience the passion that women only spoke about in hushed tones, behind closed doors, and usually only long after they were married. Her body ached to experience sensual pleasure with Forrest, her eyes hungered to see his body, to drink in his maleness. In this very yard, she was to have raised beautiful babies from their union.

She gritted her teeth against the chill of the water and the rawness of her hands, chapped by wind. Gasping, crying in the rain, Marissa's heart lurched when the sky lit up once more. He was still on the road! He was alive! Gallant, wearing the uniform she'd mended. Suddenly, a fireball whistled through the storm. Something splashed. A bullet? A cannonball?

She had to tell him she was safe. Their love was strong enough to conquer everything, even this war, but she watched in horror as the Yankee reined in his horse and turned, trotting the way he'd come, his eyes scanning the trees as if he'd heard Forrest in the brush. It was the wrong moment for her beloved to emerge in plain sight. The enemy leaned down, the night air rent by the sound of a sword drawn from his sheath. It rose high, glinting under the moon, arching as it bore down.

"Forrest!" she shrieked as the blade swung, the soldier bending. And then silence. Lightning and bullets ceased fire, plunging everything into darkness. He was dead. She knew that much. *I curse this ground*, she thought, rage swelling like the tides. *Damn women who've lived and loved on this bloodstained ground without paying this price. I hope they never find you, love. Never! Never!*

Lightning flashed. Thunder cracked.

And vaguely, Marissa realized she'd uttered the wrong curse—that the Yankees were to blame, and greedy people who would rather work the land with slaves than make do with less, but months of mere survival and feeling her heart shatter was too much! No one should enjoy Hartley House, or love, or the life Marissa was to have lived here, not until she and Forrest were reunited.

Envy—a kind of hate she'd never known—bubbled inside, so she barely noticed the next burst of fire. She felt as if she was floating above the water, no longer in her own body. She was aware of smoke, but she was numb, her skin frigid, then she realized warmth gushed from somewhere. From her shoulder, maybe? Was it blood? She wasn't sure. All she knew for certain was that Lavinia was gone. Her mama and papa, the sisters she loved. And now Forrest.

Her mind stuttered with grief. Her fingers slipped, but she kept hold of the root. If she let go, she'd never make it, and she was going to stand and fight. Oh, damn it, she would stand! For Forrest! Her hand weakened. Wind whipped her hair, and she realized a bullet had found her. She was losing blood to a salty swamp where gators circled, drawn by the scissoring movements of her legs. Suddenly, she was pummeled by wind.

And then the swirling dark waters took her.

1

New York City,
a dark, stormy February night in the present…

"DON'T RUN OFF and get yourself into trouble, Mug,"
Bridget Benning said, releasing her tawny, miniature
pug to run on the floor of the hallway before using
the point of a blue-painted fingernail to stab the doorbell of her best friend Dermott's high-rise apartment
in Battery Park City. "C'mon, Dermott," she muttered,
wondering why he'd been unavailable for weeks,
and at a time when so much was happening!

Bridget wanted his input on family matters, as well
as on which futon to buy, and she was hoping he'd take
walks with her, since March was around the corner and
without losing ten pounds, she'd never fit into spring
clothes. Now she needed him to take a trip South with
her to do some ghost-busting, something she hoped
he'd take seriously, since she couldn't go on this trip
without his support. Her parents had been living in
Hartley House when she was born, but since she'd
been a baby, Bridget had never been south of Newark,
and besides, only Dermott truly understood what Miss
Marissa's curse had done to Bridget's love life.

When Mug yipped, Bridget leaned and petted his head, cooing, "As soon as we're inside, I'll get you a doggie treat." Dermott kept a box handy for Mug. Bridget suddenly muttered, "Or not." Why wasn't her best buddy answering? "Hurry up," she whispered.

Just this week, Bridget's Granny Ginny, who lived in Florida, in Hartley House, had come to visit, reminding Bridget of Marissa's curse and how it affected women connected to Hartley House. Bridget and her sisters had never known Granny Ginny's son, who'd died young, but he was their biological father, even if Joe Benning had raised them. Because they were Hartleys by blood, the Benning girls hadn't escaped being victims of the curse. Just like her sisters, Bridget had placed the blame for her romantic failures squarely on Miss Marissa, but now, during Granny Ginny's visit, matters had taken a startling new twist.

As it turned out, this past month, Bridget had agreed to help her older sister, Edie, who owned a wedding planning business, Big Apple Brides, and who had luckily landed a celebrity client, hotel heiress, Julia Darden. Bridget, an aspiring jewelry designer who worked by day as a clerk at Tiffany's, had agreed to fashion an engagement ring, which she and Edie had hoped Julia and her fiancé would like. When Julia rejected Bridget's first design, Bridget had placed the sample ring, made with cubic zirconias, on her own finger.

When Granny Ginny arrived from Florida and saw the ring, she'd nearly swooned. According to

Granny, the ring Bridget had designed was an exact replica of the Hartley diamond, the ring Forrest Hartley had given to Miss Marissa Jennings during the Civil War, a ring supposedly still hidden in Granny's plantation house, which Granny claimed was haunted. And maybe it was. After all, without cosmic intervention, how could Bridget have designed a ring that was an exact replica of an already existing ring she'd never seen before?

Obviously, Bridget had some sort of deep psychic connection to Hartley House and the lost Hartley engagement diamond. That meant that maybe Bridget would have luck finding the original ring that was still hidden. She sucked in a sharp breath, barely able to believe any of this was happening. Just yesterday, she'd pulled Granny Ginny aside and questioned her at length. Oh, everybody in the family suspected Granny embellished the family legend; still, Bridget, Edie and Marley had suffered setbacks in love, and now Bridget wondered if something couldn't be done to reverse the curse.

"I hadn't thought so," Granny had begun. "But now that you've produced the exact replica of the Hartley diamond, everything's changed." Granny conjectured that, once the original ring was found, the ghost of Forrest Hartley could slip it onto the finger of his ghost-bride, Marissa, and then Marissa's curse on the Benning girls might be lifted. Bridget supposed that made sense, since Marissa's dream to be reunited with her fiancé would be achieved. After all, how could a woman get married without a diamond? The way Granny figured it, Bridget would be the Benning most likely to find the ring, since she'd designed one like it, and thereby seemed to have a psychic connection to it.

"C'mon, Dermott," Bridget whispered. Surely he'd help her. She didn't want to go to her own grave without marrying at least once, and for the first time, it seemed as if it was in her power to do something to reverse her bad luck with men. While all the Benning sisters were no strangers to failed romance, Dermott understood that Bridget was the sister most affected. Edie ran a close second. Despite starting her own wedding planning business, Edie rarely dated. And Marley had gotten married, but then her husband had cleaned out their joint bank account, and she'd divorced him. Now, she was dating a man named Cash Champagne who'd previously been involved with Edie, but who knew how long that would last?

Bridget just hoped she could straighten out this mess and get her own love life on track. And who could be better than Dermott? Last year, he'd even helped her apply to the *Guinness Book of World Records*, since she was convinced she'd survived more bad dates than any other single woman in America; unfortunately, Guinness had no bad dates category and didn't want to create one just for Bridget.

"Are you in the shower?" she whispered. From the street, she'd seen lights, and that meant Dermott was home. She sighed, thinking of the strange mojo in her life. This thing with the ring was odd. Bridget had shown no evidence of possessing paranormal talents before now. "Unless it counts that I knew my cabin share with the girls at the ski lodge this week was just too good to be true." She was supposed to have been there tonight with some friends, sharing Valentine champagne with dreamy men at the bar. "Yeah, right."

Stabbing the doorbell again, she tried to ignore her hurt feelings. Granted, she'd forgotten to send in her check for the share, but her girlfriends hadn't reminded her, either, and the person who'd replaced Bridget hadn't interested them before she'd gotten a part in a TV commercial. It wasn't the first time Bridget had felt she was outgrowing more superficial friends who were left over from college. Silently, she kept thinking it was time to move on to something more significant. But usually, in a girl's life, that meant marriage. And, well, Bridget, unlike most women, had a century-and-a-half-old curse in her way.

At least she could repair her self-esteem and repay her fair-weather friends by having an interesting vacation ghost-busting in Florida. Success was the best revenge, after all. Besides, she'd already arranged to take a week off from Tiffany's and she wasn't about to waste it. Probably, she wouldn't have met a cute guy at the lodge, and even if she had, that only meant something awful was destined to happen. He'd turn out to have a girlfriend, or worse, a wife…

Abruptly shaking rain from her umbrella, Bridget leaned it against the wall in the hallway, then unbelted a bright yellow raincoat she wore over a miniskirt, fishnets and snow boots. She wished Dermott would hurry! She had so much to tell him! She'd talked to him on the phone a couple of weeks ago— around the time that her sister Marley had appeared on a reality show called *Rate the Dates* with Cash Champagne, impersonating her twin, Edie. Bridget had told him Granny Ginny was visiting, but he hadn't called since then, and in twenty years she and Dermott had never gone this long without speaking. It felt like torture. Smoothing her straight, shoulder-length blond hair, Bridget wracked her brain. Was Dermott angry? She couldn't think of a thing she'd done wrong. If she'd offended him, he'd have mentioned it. He wasn't exactly Mr. Withholding. She inhaled sharply. Had he gotten hurt? Or into trouble?

But no. Dermott was a straight arrow. As steady as a rock. And he never got sick. Deciding the bell was broken, she rapped her knuckles on the door. A second later, it swung open, and as the chain caught, pulling taut, she heard a soft curse and saw the flash of a male hand.

"Who is it?" he muttered, reshutting the door long enough to slip back the chain before opening the door wide enough to see her.

"Me. Sorry." Bridget parted her pink-lipsticked lips in mild offense as her hands settled on her hips. "I've been trying to call you for weeks."

"Bridge," he said simply.

Her slackened lips parted another fraction as she registered a number of unusual things simultaneously. A half-buttoned shirt barely covered his chest, his shoes were off and he was hopping on one foot. Right before he finished pulling on a pair of fancy dress pants, she glimpsed muscular legs flashing between the shirttails and slacks.

"Did I catch you at a bad time?"

He shook his head. "Uh...no."

He was lying. Her eyes scanned over his shoulder, taking a cursory view of the familiar modern loft; open living, dining and kitchen areas were encircled by floor-to-ceiling windows. Then she registered a chocolate box on the counter of the kitchen island, a bowl of fresh strawberries and a vase of flowers.

She should have known! Dermott was as lonely as she. Had he gone so far as to get himself Valentine gifts? Once, on her birthday, when none of her friends were available, Bridget had taken herself to dinner, then ordered her own birthday cake before stopping by Dermott's to find he was throwing her a surprise party.

"I should have called," she murmured in apology, but she'd waited until the last moment, feeling sure that an attorney she'd met at an art opening in Chelsea might phone with an alternative Valentine offer. A smile played on her lips as she watched her best bud button his shirt. He'd gotten a tan on a recent trip to L.A., his dark hair was sticking straight up as if he had a Mohawk, and his five-o'clock stubble was shadowy enough that she decided the growth was probably intentional, which meant a lot had happened for him in the past weeks, also. "Are you growing a beard?"

"A little Fu Manchu thing," he admitted.

She'd seen the look in a lot of magazines, and it made sense, since he'd just spent time in L.A. "I like it. Very Ethan Hawke."

"Thanks."

"Muggy," she suddenly exclaimed, as the pug ran

past her feet and into the room. "Mug! Mu—" Stopping in midword, Bridget realized they weren't alone. A dark-haired woman, wearing a long, fancy, strapless dress, was on the other side of the kitchen island, her back to Bridget.

A woman?

What was a *woman* doing getting something from Dermott's refrigerator? Bridget's eyes widened as she got the picture. Oh, at first glance and without glasses, Bridget had thought the visitor was wearing a strapless dress, but now she recognized the brown-and-burgundy diamond-patterned fabric. It was a sheet from Dermott's bed, one Bridget had given him for Christmas.

Since it was hardly the time to analyze the lump in her throat, Bridget swallowed around it. When had Dermott gotten a girlfriend? And why hadn't he told her? Because he was career-obsessed, always taping sounds which he sold to producers of sound tracks for movies and television, or working short-term in studios with directors, mixing sound tracks, his girlfriends never lasted, and if they did for any length of time, he'd always been cagey about discussing them. If the truth be told, Bridget had never minded, since she rather liked having him to herself. Besides, her own romantic failures had provided them with plenty to talk about.

"Mug!" she repeated, knowing it was too late. "C'mere!"

Hunkering on his front paws, the dog caught a tail of the sheet between sharp teeth and tugged. Just as the woman turned, the sheet—the end of which had been tucked into ample cleavage—fell away, and Bridget found herself gaping at a naked woman holding a bottle of uncorked bubbly. Because she had trouble seeing things unless they were far in the distance, Bridget fumbled in a pocket for her glasses while the other woman wrestled the sheet from Mug who put up a fight. As Bridget slid black-framed rectangular glasses onto her nose, a figure much better-endowed than her own came into too-sharp focus. Bridget was not into women, but she had to admit the huge breasts, nipped-in waist and flaring hips were damn impressive.

After whisking the sheet from Mug and refashioning it, this time into an over-the-shoulder sarong, the other woman lifted her chin, and Bridget bit back a gasp. Just when she'd thought things couldn't get any worse, she realized she'd met this woman before.

"Carrie," she managed. As if to punctuate Bridget's pit-of-the-stomach foreboding, a hard, driving rain continued slashing against the windows and lightning flashed. Suddenly, she felt as if she was losing her grip and her own life was slipping away.

Yep. It was definitely Carrie Masterson, the most gorgeous, talked-about, perfect girl in New York. Bridget just couldn't believe this. In two weeks, she and Dermott would be walking down the aisle as attendants for their best friends, Allison and Kenneth. Everybody had been shocked when the couple asked Bridget's sister, Edie, to plan a wedding. No one knew the two of them were sleeping together, much less pregnant or buying real estate. Because Kenneth was an architect, he was building Allison the perfect home, and Bridget just knew their babies were going to be beautiful and that Allison was going to be successful in her career. Now Dermott was in bed with Carrie Masterson.

Life was steamrollering ahead for everyone but her. Oh, she wasn't about to be self-pitying, and she didn't mind working at Tiffany's, and she loved designing rings in her spare time, but she'd only recently been promoted from clerk to floor manager. By contrast, Carrie was from a wealthy prominent political family. Slender and busty where Bridget was on the flat side, dark-haired where Bridget was blond. While Bridget had been toiling at Parsons, Carrie had been busy getting a Harvard M.B.A. simply because she enjoyed the classes, and then she'd ditched all that to become a gown designer. Word had it that her father was helping her open her own shop near Stella McCartney's in the refurbished meat-packing district. Bridget sighed. She'd hoped Allison would chose her mother, seamstress Vivian Benning to make gowns and suits for Allison and Kenneth, but Allison had used Carrie instead, since they'd been friends for years.

Somehow, she found her tongue. "Sorry to… uh…interrupt."

Not bothering to hide her displeasure, Carrie sent Dermott a long-suffering glance, as if to say "I told you so," then turned on her heel and strode on long, fabulous legs toward the bedroom, calling in a lilting voice, "Good to see you, Bridget."

"You, too," Bridget managed, then added, "Muggy," in an insistent tone, since the pug was charging after the satin sheet, as if he were a tiny bull following a red cape. "C'mere, cutie."

Mug turned, his dark liquid eyes full of pleading, and she shook her head. "C'mere." When she whistled, he came running, and her heart flooded with more relief than she wanted to analyze as she scooped him into her arms. Cuddling him against her chest, she felt comforted by his heart, which was beating every bit as rapidly as hers. Ducking her chin, she smothered him with kisses.

And then she looked at Dermott again. Somehow, the apology in her mind didn't make it to her lips. With her glasses on, she certainly understood why Carrie was interested. She sucked in a breath, suddenly feeling as if she were losing her mind. She'd seen Dermott half-dressed many times, but all at once, his body had an entirely new effect. Her pulse was racing, her knees felt weak and with a jolt, she realized jealousy was coursing through her blood.

Oh, she'd always known Dermott was good-looking, with a long, rectangular face, dark, brooding eyes and thick eyebrows, but Bridget didn't think of Dermott *that* way. They'd lived next door to each other as kids, at least until Dermott's father, an actor, had gotten his big Hollywood break, and they spent plenty of time together now when Dermott wasn't in L.A. where he maintained another residence. But…

She simply couldn't believe Carrie's possessive glance. What was going on? How long had they been together? "Look," she began. "I'm sorry, Derm. I didn't know…" *That you were getting naked with Carrie.*

"No problem." Clearing his throat as if that might

help him get a better handle on the situation, Dermott squinted. "I thought you went upstate with the girls, skiing."

"Is that why you haven't called?"

The pause lasted a beat too long. "Uh…yeah."

He was lying, but why? She lunged into the story of the share mixup, then quickly said, "Are you mad at me?"

He shook his head. "No. What can I do for you?"

What can I do for you? He was talking as if they were strangers! Her throat constricted in panic. "Uh…it's nothing," she assured.

"It must be something, Bridge, or you wouldn't have come all the way to South Ferry in the rain."

He had a point, but she was starting to feel like a fool. Her friends were moving on in life, and somehow, in a way she'd couldn't quite define, she seemed stuck. Marissa's curse, no doubt! But was she really so self-absorbed that Dermott had quit telling her secrets? She hated feeling out of the loop. "Really," she managed. "It wasn't a big deal."

His eyebrows knitted. "Is something wrong, Bridge?"

Yes. No. Nothing. Everything. She'd just felt a rush of sexual attraction toward Dermott—and well, that seemed very wrong. So did the explosion of jealousy. Especially since she had no claim on Dermott except that he was her best friend. The boy next door. The man she'd come to rely on for constant consultation about her life.

"Bridget?"

She was staring at him as if she'd never seen him

before. She'd seen him with women other than Carrie, of course, and it had never bothered her, but Carrie Masterson was...

Perfect. One of the city's hot babes. *New York* magazine had even done an article about her. "Huh?"

"Is something wrong?"

"No." Except she couldn't fight this feeling that her whole world had turned upside down. Was he serious about Carrie? Was she was going to lose her best friend? Deep down, she heard a little voice say, *Carrie's the first woman he's been with whom he'd leave me for.* Except he couldn't leave Bridget, not really. They'd never even been together, not like *that.* Her eyes drifted slowly downward, and she was stunned to feel twinges in all her secret places. He really was a fine specimen of a man, sexy, with heavily lidded dark eyes that made him look as if he'd just stepped from bed.

Which he had, she reminded herself. *With Carrie.* But had they really slept together yet? Was this their first night together? Or had they been together a while?

He was peering at her. "Your family's okay?"

"Fine."

He almost smiled, and nothing more than the familiar wry upturn of his lips warmed her, taking the chill from the February storm and Carrie's cool reception. "Why are you not convincing me, Bridge?"

As she smiled back, Mug relaxed in her arms. "Really," she said. "Mom and Pop are great. Edie's wedding planning business lost some clients because people found out it was Marley, not her, who was on the *Rate the Dates* show, and apparently they're going to announce on national TV that the Bennings are victims of a wedding curse."

"Huh?"

Quickly, she filled him in on the details, that her sisters had switched places on a TV reality show, and then been discovered. "But don't worry," she added quickly. "Edie's surviving. And Marley's still dating Cash Champagne. It looks like it might be serious, but…"

"But?"

The curse was in the way. "Marley doesn't really believe things will work out between her and Cash because…well, nothing ever does for us Bennings." Experiencing an uncharacteristic chin-quiver, Bridget clamped her jaw tightly, keeping her gaze trained on Dermott's, hardly wanting to let her eyes drift, just in case they landed again on Carrie's accoutrements: chocolates, strawberries and flowers. Not that fixing her eyes on Dermott's was any better. She realized his eyes were so dark, inky, liquid…

She blew out a shaky breath. The only saving grace was that Carrie had taken the champagne.

"Hmm. So, is this about the wedding curse thing again?"

"Yeah," she admitted. "But it's a long story, and you're busy."

Something in the way he glanced over his shoulder drew her eyes to his shoulder. Why had she never noticed how broad Dermott's shoulders were before this moment—when he was checking on Carrie Masterson's movements in his apartment? His skin looked very smooth and touchable, and Bridget almost shivered when the citrus scent of it reached her. She couldn't help but say, "Have you been using that lotion I gave you? You know, the stuff I got you in Chinatown?"

As he turned toward her again, she found it both difficult to swallow and to suppress the jealous feelings she had no right to be experiencing. He nodded. "Uh…yeah."

It was probably why his skin looked so incredibly toned.

He looked torn. "Why don't you tell me what's going on?"

Obviously, she wasn't welcome, at least by Carrie, but she had come all the way downtown, and Dermott wanted to know, so… "Remember when we talked a couple of weeks ago, and I told you Granny Ginny was visiting?"

He nodded slowly, probably visualizing the woman he'd met so many times. She was five feet tall, nearing ninety, and she'd shown up on this trip dressed in a fur-collared pink coat with a matching pillbox hat.

Willfully forgetting that a naked woman was waiting in his bedroom, Bridget ducked her chin to nuzzle Mug. "She's going to be in town for a few days, so maybe you'll get a chance to see her. She just loves you."

Dermott grunted noncommittally.

In case Dermott had forgotten any details of the family history, Bridget quickly reminded him of how her own father, Jasper Hartley, had gotten drunk, fallen from a pedestal table in the Hartley House parlor and met his death, and how, during the war, Miss

Marissa Jennings had remained at Hartley House with a housekeeper named Lavinia, waiting for her fiancé's return, prefiguring the moment when, on the night they were to marry, she'd seen Forrest killed. Lavinia had been swept away by the water's currents in the swamp where she'd been hiding, and Miss Marissa had been shot.

When she was finished, Dermott said, "No offense, Bridget, but I really never understood how anybody could have known about the curse, since Miss Marissa was supposedly alone in the swamp when she uttered it."

"Granny Ginny always mentions that discrepancy," Bridget admitted, loving that Dermott had always been such an apt listener. "And to tell you the truth, even she's not really sure of the answer. All we know is the story's been handed down through generations, and that Hartley women have definitely had trouble with their love lives. Granny Ginny did say that she'd heard a distant relative called in a psychic medium once, though, who confirmed that there was a curse." Bridget paused. "And don't forget, the house is haunted."

Dermott looked at her a long moment. Seemingly deciding not to pursue that line of thought, he said, "Okay. We'll assume there's really a curse. You also said Miss Marissa got shot, but then you've said she was hit by a cannonball."

"Granny Ginny always mentions that, too," Bridget quickly said. "I guess there's some debate as to whether she was killed by a bullet or cannonball. All that's really known is that she probably died in the swamp, and Granny says that when she haunts the house, there's sometimes blood on her wedding dress." She paused. "But not all the time."

Dermott considered. "Well, unless the Union army was advancing on the property and facing a bunch of Confederates, I don't think they would have used a cannon."

"That's what I was thinking," agreed Bridget, glad he understood. "It's more likely she died from a bullet wound. Still, Granny says that when she haunts Hartley House, she sometimes carries a cannonball, but maybe that's just because it's symbolic of war, and—" Pausing, she realized Dermott was staring at her. "Hmm?"

He said, "You don't believe this, do you?"

"Nights like this make it seem possible," she offered. As her gaze shifted to the windows, she felt uncomfortable. For years, they'd talked about how the World Trade Center buildings marred the view from Dermott's high-rise. Now, both wished they'd never said such a thing. Bridget had realized too late that she'd taken the buildings for granted, too. She'd rarely visited them, and they'd been such a familiar part of the landscape since her childhood that it was hard to visualize them now. She should have paid more attention, but she'd thought the buildings would always be standing, tall and proud.

Tears stung her eyes, and she wondered what on earth was wrong with her tonight. Dermott's voice pulled her from her reverie. "You really do believe all this, huh, Bridge?"

She shrugged again. "You know I do. And anyway, Granny Ginny's a good storyteller, so whenever she talks, she makes it seem real. The main thing is—" She paused. "Did you get my voice mail?"

He nodded.

"Well, like I said, I had another talk with Granny. Now she says the curse will end if the Hartley diamond's found, and…" She held up her hand, displaying the bauble on her right ring finger. Her voice quickened. "You have to admit all this is strange, Dermott."

He eyed the bunched cluster of cubic zirconias. "Did your grandmother really say that was a replica of the engagement ring Forrest Hartley gave Marissa Jennings?"

"Not only that, but she says there's proof. A painting in the parlor of Marissa in her wedding gown, wearing this exact ring."

"And you're sure you never saw it?"

Bridget shook her head. "I haven't been there since I was a baby. When I saw the painting, I wasn't even a year old. I couldn't have remembered the ring." She surveyed Dermott. "Oh…you think she's lying."

He shrugged.

"Maybe she is," Bridget continued, "but all we have to do is go look. She says the portrait's right there, hanging in the parlor. And I know I used to sleep on the pedestal table when I was a baby, under the chandelier, so I guess I was thinking…"

"That the Hartley diamond is hidden in the chandelier?"

She'd have to see the chandelier to know, of course, but… "Isn't it possible the prisms in the chandelier look enough like this ring—" she held up her hand again "—that the original ring was hidden there?"

He looked skeptical. No...his was definitely not the excited let's-pack-our-bags-and-go-look Bridget had been hoping for. "And you saw the ring when you were under a year old, which enabled you to reproduce it when you were twenty-eight?"

"Well, I don't know," she said defensively.

"If the original ring was hidden in the chandelier, Bridge, don't you think the Yankees would have found it? Not to mention everyone else who looked, such as your grandmother?"

That was the thing about Dermott, he always made such excellent points. "Still, you'd think the Yankees would have removed the chandelier, but they didn't do that, either, and no one knows why."

"And your guess is?"

Ducking to sprinkle Mug with more kisses, she said, "Granny Ginny said Miss Marissa and Lavinia probably tried to take down the chandelier, so they could hide it, but it wouldn't budge." Her voice dropped, becoming hushed, just as Granny Ginny's did whenever she told the story. "It was as if the chandelier grew a mind all its own," she repeated, using Granny Ginny's words. "Granny Ginny said it *decided* not to leave Hartley House."

Now his lips were twitching. "Hmm. A chandelier that makes decisions. Bridge, you really can't believe this place is haunted."

"Granny swears ghosts keep her up all night."

"She's old. Maybe her mind's going."

"She's as sharp as a tack," Bridget assured. The woman was smart enough to fake swoons any time she didn't get her way, which proved she was lucid, but Bridget was worried. What if someone was trying to harm her relative? Some things Granny Ginny had said suggested people were trying to run her off her property by pretending to haunt it. Bridget suddenly sighed. "I guess I just thought you might help end the curse."

"So your love life will turn around?"

"You don't have to say it quite so bluntly."

He chuckled softly now, and she smiled in response to the familiar sound. "It's no secret. It's the overriding complaint of your life, Bridge."

"True." More than once, Dermott had pretended to be her boyfriend to dissuade Mr. Wrongs who still thought they were Mr. Rights, and at this year's Christmas party at Tiffany's, he'd even pretended they were hot and heavy, since her boss favored women with active personal lives, and she'd been in line for the promotion from clerk to floor manager, which she'd gotten. It had been a remarkable performance. All night, it had seemed as if Dermott really was her boyfriend. Everything had seemed perfect, with him in a suit, and her in a perfect black dress, and with him pouring her another glass of champagne—of exactly the brand he was supposed to be drinking with Carrie right this minute.

Her eyes slid to the bedroom door, then returned to Dermott. He really was handsome. The V of his shirt exposed thick black chest hair, and even though he'd buttoned the shirt, he hadn't done so before she'd trailed her gaze all the way down to the waistband of his slacks.

She startled. "Uh," she began quickly, pulling herself back to the matter at hand. "I was thinking, since I'm already off work all week and since I'm not going skiing…"

Dark eyes that had never looked so good before this moment widened in disbelief. "You're thinking of flying to Florida, to see if you can find the ring?"

"Well," she admitted slowly. "Maybe not flying." She wasn't proud of it, but she'd been afraid to fly since 9/11. She glanced once more toward the windows through which the Twin Towers had been visible.

"Oh." His jaw slackened. "Now, I get it."

She winced. "It was just a thought," she assured, the cubic zirconias flashing as she held out a staying hand. "Honestly, Dermott, I had no idea you were so busy. I wouldn't have come."

"You want me to drive you," he guessed.

"You were talking about taking vacation time," she defended. "And more than anyone, you have intimate knowledge of my abysmal date failures, not to mention family quirks. You've met Granny, and you're skeptical about the family myths, so I thought that might keep me in check."

His eyes were unreadable. "If you start seeing ghosts?"

"I remembered you saying you wanted to record sounds for a movie sound track," she said, rushing on, still trying not to contemplate what the sight of him, nearly naked, had done to her erogenous zones. Tucking a lock of hair behind her ear, she let her fingers linger, then tugged on her earlobe, as if that might help her hear her inner voice and jog recall. "You know, the movie that's set in the South."

He nodded. "It's a Civil War picture."

"And I was thinking…" Her words quickened. "What if there really are ghosts, Dermott, just the way Granny Ginny says? I've heard about them so often, I guess I do believe in them, but still, it's hard to imagine seeing them. What if we really heard…" She paused. "All those gunshots, cannonballs and horses…"

"I don't believe in ghosts," said Dermott flatly.

"Of course you don't," Bridget assured. "But I was just thinking…well, it might be fun to play ghostbusters. Granny Ginny says she always smells my father's whiskey and the cigars Mom made him quit smoking, and that he tracks mud and leaves the doors open." She blew out a short, determined breath. "I've been skiing before a thousand times, but I've never searched an old plantation for a ring. I just want to take one good look at the portrait and the chandelier. And like I said, wouldn't it be great if you caught sounds of real ghosts on your equipment?" Dermott owned an SUV outfitted with state-of-the-art sound equipment.

A long silence fell.

Then he said, "Let me get this straight. You need the use of my van to record possible ghost sounds?"

"I'm not sure. But it might come in handy."

"And if we go down there, find this ring and end the curse, your love life will work out?"

Put that way, it sounded ridiculous. Nevertheless, she nodded. "That's what Granny Ginny said."

"And you'll marry somebody?"

"That's ambitious. Sex would be good." *Maybe just a date on Valentine's day*, she thought, but wasn't about to call attention to Dermott's situation again with Carrie Masterson. "I could start with sex," she joked, the smile growing tight when she realized she was imagining having that sex with Dermott, "and then work my way up."

Outside, a loud thunderclap sounded, claiming her attention, and she watched as lightning crossed a darkened window. Straight in front of her, she could see the waters of the Hudson swell against empty slips at the Manhattan Yacht Club, and to the right, the space where the Towers had been. She tried to visualize how they'd looked, but she simply couldn't, just as she couldn't exactly envision how Dermott had looked to her before five minutes ago when she'd found Carrie naked in his apartment. Now, he seemed like a completely different man.

Suddenly whimpering, Mug burrowed in the hollow of her shoulder. "Look," she managed. "I'd really better go."

And then Dermott scratched his jaw and said the last thing Bridget expected, proving that he was still her best bud. "I've got a few days off. Then I'm in L.A. for a long weekend."

She squinted. "You are?"

He nodded. "My agent got me a gig with a new indie director. They want me to go over some of the sound mix and help re-edit it. Right after that, we're in Kenneth and Allison's wedding. But between now and the L.A. gig…" He sighed. "Okay, Bridge. I'll go pack. What time should I pick you up in the morning?"

Her heart soared in a way she'd never imagined it could. Even though Carrie Masterson was here, Dermott was going to help her. "How about seven?"

"EVERYBODY warned me!" Carrie exploded a moment later, her dark hair bristling as it flew around her shoulders.

Dermott, who was particularly sensitive to sounds, listened to the flapping sheet as she snapped it from her body, then to the soft rustle as she reached for her bra and panties. Somehow, it didn't help that she'd been wearing one of the sheets Bridget had given him for Christmas. "Don't go, Carrie," he said, but he knew the words were useless. She was flying around his bedroom like one of Bridget's poltergeists. What a night! He'd been tied up at work, Carrie had wanted to give him a final fitting of the suit for Allison and Kenneth's wedding, and it was raining, so he'd been afraid she'd get stranded, which was why he'd told the doorman to let her inside his apartment.

"A wedding fitting on Valentine's day?" the doorman had questioned, which should have given Dermott a hint.

"It's the city that never sleeps," he'd returned, not giving it a second thought. He'd been looking forward to seeing Carrie, too. Gorgeous, rich, talented and ambitious, she was the perfect New York woman. Previously, they'd flirted to survive the awkward moments when she'd checked the fit of his pants, and Dermott had known she was interested, just not *this* interested.

Before he'd arrived, she'd hidden flowers, champagne and chocolates, and while he'd changed in the bathroom into the suit pants, she'd changed, also, and he'd come out to find her naked.

It had been the perfect opportunity to get Bridget out of his system, a project he'd given renewed effort for the past two weeks, ever since she'd called, saying her Granny Ginny was coming to town. Walking swiftly to Carrie, he'd grabbed her hand and led her to the bedroom, do not pass Go.

"I was afraid I was taking too big a risk," she'd whispered.

"Oh, no," he'd assured, hurriedly starting to shuck his slacks and unbutton his shirt, which was the exact moment when Bridget *would* start ringing the buzzer, in a way too insistent to ignore.

"Bridget and I are just friends," he said now, frustrated since Carrie was leaving. For the past few days he'd been working his tail off, traveling around the Manhattan shoreline, trying to pick up background recordings of traffic sounds and seagulls flying over the Hudson that wouldn't sound canned. Finally, he'd gotten something that satisfied a director after he'd mixed it into a sound track for a TV pilot. He was tired, but if Bridget hadn't blown the deal, Carrie would have been the perfect nightcap.

As she finished buttoning her blouse, he could hear her nails scrape on fabric. She turned a skirt around on her waist to get a better look at the zipper while she pulled it up, then reversed the skirt once more. She glanced up. "Oh, really?"

"Yes, really."

He could hardly tell Carrie, but when Bridget had started babbling about the curse again, he'd realized it was truly hopeless. Nothing was ever going to change between them. He'd never denied that he was in love with her. Everything about Bridget Benning heated his blood, and for years, he'd bided his time, waiting for her to come around. He'd even told her on a few occasions, but she'd only laughed off his advances, never taking them seriously, not even when he'd assured her his emotions weren't to be toyed with.

Meantime, refusing to live like a lovelorn pup, he'd dated other people, and he'd been focused on work, building a résumé in his field, but now he was successful, which meant he got a lot of social opportunities he had to start taking. Today marked the fourteenth day since he'd last spoken to Bridget. Feeling more determined than at previous times when he'd distanced himself, he was actually counting days. For two weeks, he'd caroused in clubs and called countless numbers scribbled on cocktail napkins.

Couldn't Bridget see through her own delusions? Didn't she realize how mercilessly she'd come on to him at the Christmas party at Tiffany's? She'd needed a date, and he'd played it to the hilt, since her boss favored employees who were interested in settling down, but she'd given as good as he, and it had been difficult—hanging on to her every word, stroking her neck, murmuring in her ear. He'd watched in satisfaction as nipples he'd longed to stroke stiffened under a hot little black dress she'd worn just to drive him mad. He'd whispered, "Why don't we ever get together, Bridge?"

She'd only laughed—a soft, airy musical lilt that had always driven him crazy—and then she'd elbowed him, as if what he'd said was ridiculous. "We're best friends."

He'd modulated his voice, trying to sound more casual than he'd felt, hating these moments that had surfaced so often over the years. "Friends can't be lovers?"

She'd shaken her head adamantly. "It never works out."

"I thought you said your love life never works out, anyway." He'd forced himself to laugh.

She'd chuckled, and that was the end of the conversation.

Carrie's voice brought him back to the present. "Allison said you're always at that woman's beck and call," she said, a pair of black tights whispering on her thighs as she pulled them on. "You never date."

"I date a lot of women."

"Not for long, not seriously."

It was more true than he wanted to admit. "Bridget only relies on me to pick her up after her own failed romances."

Carrie was slipping her feet into flats, generating a soft brushing sound. "Which is why you're going on vacation with her at the drop of a hat?"

Obviously, *his* love life was going to remain cursed until Bridget was a closed chapter. This gorgeous woman had been right in front of him, naked and holding a bottle of champagne. "Only because I'm going to tell Bridget we can't be friends."

Whisking her coat from a chair, Carrie swirled it around her shoulders, then surveyed him. "Are you serious?"

"Yes." He'd tried to cool it with Bridget over the years, and for just this reason. It never worked. While he suspected Bridget felt attraction for him, she hid it so well, even from herself. *Especially* from herself. "She relies on me," he continued simply. Bridget needed him, but he was going to have to take some action. "She denied it, but I think she really believes in the ghosts her grandmother says are haunting her house."

"I overheard."

"Maybe if I help her sort this out, she'll get over the idea that she's cursed. She dates somebody new every week," he added, just in case Carrie misunderstood his intentions. "So, it's clear she's not interested in me, except as a friend. Maybe one of those guys will work out for her, and she'll learn to be less reliant on me."

Carrie headed toward the front door. Once there, she turned. "You actually seem to believe what you're saying."

"What's not to believe?"

When she rolled her eyes, his heart hardened. He really was sick of this. Carrie Masterson was hardly the first woman to object to his relationship with

Bridget. Every woman he'd dated expected to find him in bed with her—and never had. Funny, he thought now, most were less threatened by the idea of him and Bridge hitting the sheets than by their twenty-year friendship. That's what should have unsettled them. But he was tired of playing the best friend. He was ready to give her up.

He eyed Carrie. She was the kind of woman who could have anyone she wanted—and she'd chosen him. She could make a nice home for a man, she was talented and sexy as hell. Once more, Bridget was helping him blow it. "Bridget and I have been close for years," he found himself saying. "So, I need time."

"To end the friendship, so you can move on?" Carrie kept her eyes on his. More softly, she said, "She's getting in your way, Dermott." As she opened the door, she added, "I almost believe you. Okay. One week. I'll call your cell while you two are gone." She flashed a smile, her dark eyes holding the promise of a future if he let go of Bridget. "You know, monitor your trip, Dermott." Her eyes hardened. "But you need to put an end to this. It's at a stalemate for you. No sex. No progression. Just her being a buddy, when other women want to give you so much more, Dermott."

With that, Carrie swept across the threshold; the click of the door seemed to resound in the silence. Alone, Dermott pushed away a recollection of the shocked look on Bridget's face when she'd caught him with his pants down. She'd actually fumbled in her bag, looking for her glasses to get a better look at Carrie before she realized they'd already met. Yeah, Bridget's behavior had communicated sexual interest, but then, he'd seen that look at the Tiffany's Christmas party, too, and on a thousand other occasions.

Carrie was right. Bridget would never allow that part of the relationship to progress. And the way he held on to the friendship made him look like a fool, not that he really cared what other people thought. Still, Carrie had underestimated his frustration. Bridget hadn't been good for him. While most women treated him like a sexy male—Carrie was hardly the first he'd found naked—Bridget made *him* feel like a ghost, and while her clear blue eyes might haunt him, he wasn't going to let her ruin any more of his chances.

Yeah, he was blowing out this torch. No matter what Bridget said or did, and no matter how much she tempted him, he wasn't going to let her ignite any false hopes again. Yeah. Bridget Benning could rub her thin, sexy body all over him...she could even pull down his zipper, slip a warm hand inside and...

He sucked in a breath. Anyway, the point was, he wouldn't give in to temptation. When they parted company a final time, he'd miss her like hell. He'd love her forever. But he had to move on. So, he was going to the Sunshine State, and by the time he returned, he and Bridget, just like the supposed ghosts of Hartley House, would be a closed chapter belonging to history.

2

Hartley House,
a dark and stormy night forty-eight hours later…

GETTING Dermott into bed wasn't as easy as Bridget anticipated, but ever since she'd seen Carrie naked in his apartment, she'd decided she and her best buddy should at least *try* sex together. If they didn't, they'd always wonder about it. Hadn't they voiced attraction before, as Dermott had at the Christmas party? What if he got serious about Carrie, got married and never spent a night exploring the attraction forbidden in his friendship with Bridget?

Last night, when they'd stopped at a hotel in North Carolina, Bridget had planned to make her move, but Dermott had quickly retired to the private room he'd insisted on having to call Carrie. Not that it was necessary. Carrie called every five minutes. So had Bridget's sisters. Edie was worried, since she was losing business at Big Apple Brides, and Marley kept teasing Bridget, asking if she'd resolved the curse yet, saying she didn't want to lose the man she was dating, Cash Champagne. Other than that, Dermott had taped sounds at most of their stops, concentrating on those indigenous to the South. It was almost as if he was using work as an excuse not to talk.

"That's weird," Dermott said now, just as they turned off the main road onto the shell driveway leading to Hartley House. He'd hunched over the steering wheel to spin the radio dial. "All I'm getting is static."

"Definitely an omen." She peered into the darkness as the last finger of twilight glimmered, hardly caring about finding music on the radio since the house was bound to materialize soon. As she dug into a pocket for her glasses and put them on, Mug leaped from Dermott's lap to hers. "Isn't this exciting Muggy Puggy?" she cooed. "We're almost at the haunted house. Do you think we're going to see Dracula? Or Frankenstein? What do you think of this awful thunderstorm? Is it an omen?"

Wagging his tawny tail furiously, Mug spun in circles on her lap. Along with fishnet stockings and black, pointy-toed "witch shoes," which she'd worn specifically for the occasion, she'd put on a sunny yellow jumper; because it was made of vinyl, she figured she could wash off Mug's muddy paw prints once they got inside. "I'm beat," she offered, rolling her head on her shoulders to work out the kinks.

Peering through the deluge battering the windshield, Dermott said, "Me, too."

They'd gotten a start later than the appointed 7:00 a.m. time on the previous day, which left Bridget wondering just what Dermott and Carrie had been doing all that night, especially since Dermott had been driving like a bat out of hell—as if he couldn't wait to get back to New York and Carrie. A couple of hours ago, when they'd finally hit the two-block town of Big Swamp, Florida, they'd picked up groceries and eaten at a greasy spoon diner next to a motel that looked eerily similar to Norman Bates's place in the movie *Psycho.* Just thinking of the motel, Bridget felt a sudden chill, as if a cool draft had swept through the SUV's interior.

"Everybody at Nancy's Diner said Granny Ginny's place is really haunted," she found herself saying conversationally.

Dermott approximated a Transylvanian accent, announcing, "I'm going to suck your blood."

She hummed sexily. "Sounds promising."

He shot her a quick, startled glance, then stared through the windshield again, unwilling to acknowledge the flirtation. She sighed. Dermott had never been less fun, and she just didn't understand it. It was as if he'd decided to put up some impenetrable guard, to protect himself from her, almost as if he'd guessed she had sex on her mind.

At least he'd been talking with a Transylvanian accent, which was amusing. In fact, he'd been doing so when they'd entered the restaurant in Big Swamp, so she'd barely noticed the stir they created. Only after they were seated had Bridget realized she was the only woman wearing a dress, much less a micromini with fishnets. Here, denim and flannel ruled. And when she and Dermott had asked Nancy, the owner, who also doubled as a waitress, to further describe grits and red gravy, everybody had doubled over laughing. At least until they'd realized where the fish-out-of-water couple was heading. Then they'd wheeled around on orange stools to stare, shaking their heads as if to say Bridget and Dermott were out of their freaking minds.

"You can't spend the night!" Nancy warned, concern in her eyes. "Didn't Ginny mention the place is haunted?"

During the meal, Dermott had tried to convince Bridget that the haunting was just a local legend which helped people, Granny Ginny included, to pass the time. Now she was beginning to hope so. It was spooky out here. Listening to the wipers move sludge and leaves across the windshield, she took off a black baseball cap, tossed it to the dashboard and tilted her head so that a ponytail fell over her shoulder and down her back. Mug turned and placed his paws on the dash, to get a better look through the rain-sluiced windows.

She still couldn't see much, so she cast a glance toward Dermott again, wondering how tonight was going to play out. Would they have sex? And what had happened, anyway? One minute Dermott was her best bud, but on Valentine's night, after she'd left his apartment, she'd dreamed the most down-and-dirty sex dream she'd ever had about a man. A paradigm shift, she thought. That's what they called it. Suddenly, the world had spun on its axis—and now Dermott was the hottest thing she'd ever laid eyes on. Very definitely, strange mojo was at work.

In the dream, she'd seen Dermott open the door to his apartment again, and once more, she'd glimpsed the dark curling hairs trailing on the hard, bunched muscles of his thighs, and then she'd imagined he wasn't pulling on the slacks, but taking them off instead—and not for Carrie, but for her. Not that she'd been able to prod Dermott into having a conversation about the other woman.

"Why do you care about whether it's serious between me and Carrie?" he'd asked last night.

"I always tell you about my boyfriends," she'd pointed out.

"Right," he'd said. "But I don't kiss and tell."

Was that all he'd done with Carrie? "Oh, please. You say that as if you're morally superior."

He'd laughed. "Draw your own conclusions."

Yes, his refusal to be forthcoming was a bad sign, she decided. She always told him about her boyfriends because they didn't mean anything and, on the basis of that, she had to conclude that Carrie Masterson was important. She blew out a long sigh now, wondering if magical forces would really come into her life on this trip.

Of course, lust was a factor in how she felt. Dermott looked better than any man had a right to. His hair was mussed, his five-o'clock shadow had moved toward six or seven o'clock, becoming darker and more scraggly. Loose black jeans and a V-necked T-shirt she'd given him on his last birthday hugged his body, looking chic. Sucking in a breath, she wondered if she hoped she'd find the nerve to proposition him. She imagined herself asking him if he wanted to have sex with her. Then she imagined herself simply reaching down and cupping her hand over his jeans fly. *Why not?*

"See if you can find some music, Bridge."

She imagined his unbuttoned shirt, the tufts of unruly dark hair calling for her fingers. Shifting Mug in her lap, she squinted through the darkened windshield and spun the radio dial. "Ghosts," she explained when she found only static. "Don't they interfere with radio signals?"

Dermott nodded. "Wait until we get indoors. Maybe the insides of the phone have been removed, too."

She chuckled. "Like in a *Twilight Zone* episode, cutting us off from the outside world?"

"Exactly."

Her laughter tempered when she thought about their experience at the diner again. In a long line of pickup trucks, Dermott's SUV had stood out, and as soon as people had discovered they were visiting Hartley House and driving an SUV containing recording equipment, they'd decided she and Dermott had come for the sole purpose of taping ghosts. The people in the diner, of course, would never guess what was really on Bridget's mind when she thought of spending the night with Dermott in a haunted house.

The closer they got, the more overgrown the driveway became, and as Dermott slowed, she became more conscious of the sound of shells crunching under the tires. Even though they were inside, she ducked instinctively as they traveled beneath a thick canopy of trees; Granny's place had gone so long untended that branches were scraping the SUV's roof. The lawn's massive trees, far larger than any she'd seen in Central Park, had gnarled, twisted roots that would have done Wes Craven proud. Her eyes followed them as they advanced like marching spiders.

Her breath suddenly caught. "There it is!"

Mug went still in her lap, standing at attention, his paws resting on the dashboard as the house loomed out of the darkness like a giant, but possessing none of the usual features that made a house look scary, such as turrets or a widow's walk or nearby waves that crashed against a rocky coastline. There was, however, a swamp that opened into tidewaters, and lightning that flashed between trees, illuminating a white-painted brick house that was very square and imposing; climbing ivy framed the windows and crawled into gutters, sending a promising quiver through her. The upstairs windows didn't disappoint, either, gaping down like vacant, empty eyes. A columned veranda encircled the ground floor.

She inhaled sharply. "The door's open, Dermott!"

Having seen the house now, he sounded uncharacteristically pensive. "Sure is."

"Should I call the police?"

He paused. "It couldn't hurt."

Swallowing hard, barely able to believe how haunted the house really looked, Bridget punched in 911. The phone rang and rang. Finally a woman picked up and said, "What can I do you for, hon?"

Bridget shot Dermott a glance. "Uh...I'm in Big Swamp," she began, "visiting a relative, Ginny Hartley. And, well, we got to the house and the door's wide-open." She paused. "Have I reached 911, or is this a wrong number?"

"Sure have, honey," returned the woman. "Trouble

is, the sheriff's on his dinner break, and when he gets back, I already promised Mary Lou Bidden he'd come over and help shut her windows, to keep out the storm. Her house is over a century old and the wood sticks."

"I see," Bridget managed as Dermott brought the SUV to a halt under what was probably a willow tree; it was still raining hard and Bridget could scarcely see five feet in front of the vehicle now. Her heart hammering, she wondered if she was really about to see a replica of the ring she wore. *Impossible. Dermott's right. The old family legends are just stories spun for the amusement of country people on rainy days.*

A beep had sounded on the line. The woman said, "I've got another call, but don't worry, the sheriff will check your premises in two shakes of a lamb's tail."

As Bridget turned off the phone, Dermott switched off the ignition, and then they both peered at the house. "The cops are coming no time soon, huh?" asked Dermott.

"Guess not." As she hugged Mug nearer, the enclosed space of the SUV felt claustrophobic. Suddenly, she was conscious of the silence left in the absence of the motor, and of Dermott's good looks. Unbidden, she thought of the last time she'd visited the place where the Trade Centers had stood. Twining her fingers through the chain link fence, she'd stared at the workers and said a silent prayer for those who'd died, as she always did. And then she'd tried to remember exactly what the buildings had looked like, but no matter how hard she'd tried, she simply couldn't. She'd felt just terrible.

Now a lump formed in her throat, and even though

she knew she was being ridiculously maudlin, she wondered if she could ever forget Dermott. He, too, had been a daily part of her life for so long; what if he was gone and she couldn't visualize his face?

He was looking at her curiously. "Is something the matter, Bridge?"

No, except that I'm feeling strangely grateful for the pictures I have of you, just in case you're serious about Carrie Masterson and I never see you again. "Uh...no." She glanced toward the house, sucking in a sharp breath. "Granny Ginny said the ghosts open the doors, especially Jasper. You know, my biological dad. Her son."

His laughter lifted her mood. "I can't believe you let that crazy old lady get to you, Bridge." His expression softened. "Still, you really do blame the curse for everything that goes wrong in your love life, so I can see why you'd want to believe her."

Bridget didn't make the connection. "Huh?"

"Well, if Granny's telling the truth, you can find the ring and get on with your life, just like you said."

Put that way, it sounded so unlikely. But Granny Ginny was a born storyteller, and when she spoke, Bridget could almost see skinny Lavinia strutting around the parlor, bossing Miss Marissa around.

"Probably Granny Ginny forgot to close the door," he assured. "We'll find some warm, happy field mice that got inside. Maybe a raccoon. Or a skunk."

"Oh, fabulous."

Dermott's lips were twitching, making him look even sexier in the dark, his smile just a quick flash of perfect teeth, his eyes catching light that had no source but himself. "You're really scared, aren't you?"

"Of course not." But she was, just a little.

Swiftly reaching behind him, he grabbed a flashlight, and gripped his duffel. "That decides it. We're not waiting for the police. I'm going to prove to you that the only thing to fear is fear itself, sweetheart. We're going in."

"Ghost-busters unite," she agreed, suddenly giggling, determined to push away the strange feelings warring inside her. So what if she'd taken Dermott for granted? Wasn't that the case in most long-term friendships? "It's a long run to the house."

"I pulled as close as I could."

She peered through the rain. "Ready, Mug?"

The tawny tail went wild, tapping her arm on its trajectory, and as Mug released staccato barks, Bridget reached for her own bag and pulled up the hood of a dark cape. "Did you bring an umbrella?"

"Nope, but I've got a flashlight."

As he grabbed it, she tucked Mug securely under her arm, uttered another quick, "Ghost-busters unite," then lunged through the open door. Her black, pointy-toed boots splashed into a puddle, and she squealed as icy water hit her calves, then she slammed the door, keeping her eyes on the weak, watery beam of light coming from behind her and bobbing as Dermott jogged. "I thought it was hot and sunny in Florida," she called over her shoulder, her open mouth catching salty rain.

"Not at night in February."

"And in a haunted house," she reminded, calling the words over her shoulder and batting her eyes against the rain pelting her face. "So much for my

Florida tan! I guess the girls I didn't go skiing with won't turn green with envy."

His voice was closer behind her now, comforting when it caught with concern. "Was it really that big a deal?"

"It mattered," she said, quoting something her mom, Viv Benning, had often said to her, "but not that much." Her mom had always encouraged her to feel her emotions fully, never denying them, but Bridget hadn't been taught to dwell in the negative, either. More than her sisters, she had a loving heart that made it hard to let go of relationships when it was time. Now she called, "Those girls are thoughtless. I need new friends."

"Do they have to be living?"

The comment hit the spot. He always knew just what to say. A little joke, a nice spoonful of encouragement. Nothing too heavy-handed. "Lavinia, Miss Marissa and Jasper will do fine."

Tossing her head as she reached the porch, she threw back her hood and leaned so Mug could skitter across unkempt floorboards, covered with leaves and twigs, one of which he appropriated, holding it possessively between his teeth.

Bridget paused. "Uh…you first. Do the guy thing."

He stared at her. "Carry you across the threshold?"

The thought did strange things to her heart, making it miss a beat, then come back doubly strong, hammering. "Uh…no. The ghost bride might not like that." But why had he even suggested it? Fleetingly, she wondered if the strange vibrations around the house were drawing him closer. "I just meant for you to go first. You know," she added. "Smite the ghosts."

As Dermott stepped across the threshold into a foyer, she realized the fading evening light hadn't penetrated the interior, and she hunched her shoulders instinctively as she watched him advance, shining the wavering beam into a room at their left.

Mug, who was still at the threshold, whimpered. "Mug won't come in. I think he's scared. Do you think it's a sign…"

Dermott's voice floated in the darkness. "That ghosts are here?"

"They say dogs are more sensitive than people."

"Thanks."

"Nothing personal." Whistling, she leaned down and snapped her fingers. "C'mon, Muggy Puggy. Why, everybody in here knows you're cuter than Brad Pitt, even the ghosts. Come to Bridgy-widgy!"

Dermott snorted. "Did you just say 'Bridgy-widgy?'"

"It worked," she pointed out as Mug lunged toward her. Using her bent knee as a running board, he dived into her arms, the stick still between his teeth. "Anyway, you love it," she added. And he did. Her lengthy one-sided monologues with Mug were ludicrous, but always amused Dermott.

Shutting the door, she stepped more fully inside, crossing the threshold from the foyer, then she crinkled her nose, her heart stuttering. "Do you smell that?"

"Dust?"

"Cigars and whiskey. Granny Ginny said she can always smell them." She lowered her voice. "It's Jasper."

"Whoo-oo-oo," Dermott singsonged, then he added in a mock scary fright-night voice as the thin yellow beam blinked out, "I am the ghost of Jasper Hartley." Just as she ogled the dark, trying to locate Dermott, he blindsided her, grabbing her around the waist and whirling her in the dark, making her squeal.

"You're scaring Mug!" she protested, but not before she'd registered the feel of Dermott's body against hers—the brush of a hip against her buttock, of a fly against her pelvis, the hard wall of his chest against her breasts, which suddenly ached. Just as the quick flex of possessive fingers left her belly, she shuddered in a way that had nothing to do with the house; that's when she decided she needn't worry. Whenever she got around to propositioning Dermott, he'd go for it. Definitely. Secretly, he'd been as curious as she for years…right?

Pushing away thoughts of the night they were sure to spend together, she blew out a shaky breath. "I want to find the parlor," she managed. "The portrait and the chandelier."

"We will," he said, then paused. "Here."

She heard a click before a thin light leaked into the room; blinking, she realized the illumination came from a converted oil lamp, wired for electricity. "Nice antiques," she murmured, squinting.

"I ought to find the fuse box in case the storm gets worse."

"Granny Ginny says there's a fire box full of wood on the back porch," she informed him. "All the fireplaces work."

"A fire sounds good."

The idea of lying in front of one with him sounded even better. Once more, she felt her insides get strangely tight and she took a steadying breath. In front of her was a red-carpeted staircase. To her left, Dermott was exploring an old-fashioned drawing room that gave the impression of Victorian opulence: hardwood floors covered by an Oriental rug, over-stuffed sofas, a leather bridge table, standing lamps with gold shades hemmed with fringe. Daguerreo-type photographs were on every table, and in one corner was an antique spinning wheel.

Heavy red velvet drapes were tied back, held by thick sashes, and the blinds beneath were half raised to expose the lower half of the window. Bridget gasped, then realized the movement she'd seen was her own reflection. When lightning flashed once more, she caught a glimpse of the yard beyond. It was filled with trees—what seemed to be an orange grove—and branches crooked every which way in the darkness, looking foreboding. Shaking her head to clear it of confusion, she told herself that Dermott was right. She'd been listening to Granny Ginny's stories since birth, and now her mind was running wild. "I can't help but wonder if someone's been try-ing to scare her," she suddenly said, forcing herself to be practical.

"Who? Your grandmother?"

She nodded. "When she came to visit, she seemed relieved, almost as if she didn't want to come back here, Dermott, even though it's her home. And if there really aren't ghosts…then she's definitely reacting to something else. Something she's afraid of. I asked her a lot of questions…"

"And she's how old?"

At that, Bridget smiled. "No one's had the nerve to filch her driver's license and look. In her eighties, I'd imagine. Still, she really is as sharp as a tack."

"Maybe she's just lonely."

"Maybe," she returned as he patted one of the sofas, soliciting dust particles that spiraled into the musty air; she set Mug down again, so he could run.

"I take it cleaning isn't Granny Ginny's strong suit," remarked Dermott.

Glancing behind her, she inhaled sharply. Muddy footprints led into the room. "Look, Derm. Tracks."

Dermott cracked up. "Those are *our* footprints."

"Oh," she managed, feeling shaken. Of course they were. What was she thinking? The long drive must have gotten to her. Still… "There are more than two sets," she forced herself to point out, knowing she sounded like a fool.

"Your grandmother's," he reminded.

Relief washed over her, but then she squinted, thinking of Ginny who was so small boned. "Those prints are *big*, Dermott."

He followed her gaze, his dark brows knitting before he sent her a devilish grin. "The ghost of bigfoot?"

Glancing toward her bag, she decided she didn't want to haul things upstairs before they did some exploring. "C'mon," she said, jerking her head to the right, the direction in which Granny Ginny had said they'd find the parlor. "I'm tired, but I can't wait until tomorrow to look at that portrait or the chandelier." Her heart hitching with excitement, she peered into another drawing room that seemed to open onto other rooms. "Rooms inside rooms," she murmured darkly.

"Well, I don't think anyone's here," he said. "Not even mice. I'll bet your grandmother just forgot to close the door. I'm sure it won't hurt to keep looking around before the police come." He smiled. "I'll do the guy thing and complete a bogeyman check with you."

"You guy, you," she teased.

"Then I'll do the girl thing and put away our groceries."

"Don't forget the lumberjack thing," she suggested, her mood lightening further. "You could build us a fire."

"You sure know how to work a man."

Realizing they were actually flirting, she felt the shaky sensation that had been plaguing her since they'd left New York: She was breathless, weak-kneed, and her heart was missing beats. Leaning as he came toward her, she took the risk, reached and grabbed his hand. In the brief silence that ensued, she could hear the rain slashing against the window-panes and rustling in the leaves as the wind whistled around the house. She held her breath, waiting for him to pull away, but he didn't...

Tugging him toward the darkened area of the downstairs, she wondered how many times she'd been alone with Dermott. Easily thousands. Maybe even tens of thousands. But right now, with him bumping her side in the inky blackness of this creaky old house, she was so much more conscious of him.

She could feel the skin of his palm quiver and sense the lightning-fast rush of blood racing through him, as well as hear the shallowness of his breath and the brush of denim as he walked.

She wolf-whistled. "C'mon, Mug." She glanced behind them, relieved to see Mug running at a full gallop until he was right behind them, nipping at their heels. As Dermott trained the flashlight around the room, she located lamps and switched them on. "Cigars," she said again. "And whiskey."

"It's strong in here," Dermott agreed, only now dropping her hand, leaving her fingers feeling bereft.

She shivered. "Strange mojo," she whispered, finding another lamp in yet another room and flicking it on. She gasped. "This is the parlor!"

Her eyes found the chandelier first. It was huge. Overwhelming. A three-tiered affair, it had never been wired for electricity and looked more like an oversize wedding tiara than a light fixture. The prisms were larger than any Bridget had ever seen, heavier and of more intricately cut glass, shaped like falling teardrops. "I'd love to see it lit," Bridget said breathlessly, staring at the many-sided crystals that were as bright and elegant as the diamonds she dealt with every day at Tiffany's. Countless pale yellow tapers nestled in the prisms, and Bridget was completely taken by the sheer romance of it. "We've got to light the chandelier and see how it looks."

"I'm game," agreed Dermott.

She imagined candlelight shining through all the dangling prisms, making them look like holograms. Even now, touched by nothing more than a weak lamp from the opposite side of the room, she could see the light refracting, sending out rays of astonishing color—deep pink, silver-blue and emerald-green.

She shifted her gaze, not seeing the portrait on the first pass of her eyes, just a green rug hemmed with fringe that Granny Ginny said had been added to the room long after the war, and a fireplace that made her jaw slacken. The rock slabs were grainy gray, but shot through with veins of color that complemented those emitted by the chandelier. "The rock came from a local quarry."

Dermott wasn't listening. Instead of responding, he whispered, "I'll be damned."

"Hmm?" Her eyes had settled on the room's centerpiece, the pedestal table her grandmother had told her she'd slept on in her bassinet as a baby. Its clawed feet ran across the green carpet, looking just as gnarled as the tree roots in the yard. She was thinking she could stand on it and look at the prisms when Dermott said, "I don't believe this. Look. The painting."

When she followed his gaze, she inhaled sharply. "The ring." Pausing, she took in the portrait of Miss Marissa Jennings, her heart lurching. When she found her voice, she said, "Granny told me the rings were exactly alike…" But she hadn't really believed. Sure enough, though, the dark oil portrait of Marissa, wearing her wedding dress, was opposite the fireplace, and on Marissa's finger, she wore a ring that exactly matched Bridget's.

She studied the long, slender-fingered hand extending from beneath a lace cuff. The index finger was extended, ostensibly to point at a book in her lap, but really to call attention to the ring. *One more paradigm shift*, she thought. Oh, she always got sucked into Granny's stories, but here was proof they were true.

Dermott came to stand behind her, the hard wall of his chest brushing her back. Time seemed to stand still. His breath was so close she could feel it on her cheeks, and it smelled enticing and sweet. She could smell his skin, too, a light citrus scent that wafted from warm flesh. How many times had Dermott brushed against her without soliciting this response? A thousand? Swallowing hard, wondering what on earth was happening to her, she turned her attention to the painting again, and the ring. It really was something to behold. "How could this be…" she whispered.

"There must be a reasonable explanation," he murmured, but this time, even Dermott was shaken.

"And in the picture, she seems…so alive," Bridget continued, shock turning her voice husky. It was as if Miss Marissa could walk right off the canvas. "She was beautiful." With an oval face, dark eyes and very red lips, all set in china-white skin. The wedding gown her sisters had sewn was pure eye candy. "Edie would love this," she added, thinking of how such a dress might look hanging in the display windows of Big Apple Brides.

"Pretty," Dermott said, as if he was trying to change the subject, giving himself time to process that the ring on Bridget's finger really did match that worn by Marissa.

That was another thing she liked about Dermott, Bridget thought, watching him take in the dress.

He'd always understood her affinity for clothes. Most guys would tease her. Oh, they loved to look at the outfits she put together and the wild jewelry she designed for herself, but whenever she pored over magazines, or stopped to admire store windows, or dragged them into jewelry shops, they would subtly put her interest down, as if fashion were the domain of women, and therefore beneath them. Not so, Dermott. "The ring," she whispered once more.

He blew out a breath. "Pretty weird. But I still say there's some explanation. Even though you were a baby last time you were in this room, maybe you really did remember, somehow…"

"And reproduced this ring design from my forgotten memory of it in the portrait?" Doubtful, she thought, feeling shaky. Just standing here, she could feel Granny Ginny's story coming to life once more. She could picture Lavinia with her hair wrapped in a kerchief, and her dark eyes flashing with fire as she mixed herbs and potions. "Lavinia made voodoo dolls," she reminded.

"I hope you're not mad at me."

"One pin," she assured, "and a man's a goner. She supposedly made potions, too…"

"For love…"

Just hearing him say the word made her blood quicken. Wow. Too bad Lavinia wasn't around to mix up a potion tonight. Bridget became aware of the night beyond the windows again, of how it seethed with dark vegetation and animals in the swamps. It was the perfect evening to build a fire and cuddle close. Suddenly, unbidden, her heart twisted inside her. "It's such a shame she died that night. She...really loved him."

"Forrest?"

She nodded, eyeing satin folds the painter had made look so real, then a high collar that showed off Miss Marissa's slender neck. The bodice was tailored and flattering. Suddenly, Bridget blinked, feeling a tremor in her own hand when her eyes settled on the ring again. She glanced down at the cluster of connected cubic zirconias that cascaded like a waterfall on her own ring finger. She could only shake her head. "I just don't know," she managed. "Even if a baby could remember this painting, what are the chances she'd remember the ring in any detail?"

"It makes as much sense as your other theory."

"Which was?"

"That you were left sleeping in a bassinet on the table when you stared up and saw the ring hidden in the chandelier." He eyed the light fixture, a smile tilting his lips. "Although I have to say, it definitely outclasses most baby mobiles I've seen."

"Since when did you become a baby-mobile expert?"

"Since never."

Her lips remained parted, and suddenly, she recalled all the conversations they'd had about the future. He didn't talk too much about kids, but he loved his nephews, his sister's sons, and expected to have his own someday. He dreamed of living between New York, where he'd grown up, and L.A., where his family was, not to mention movie work. So many nights, they'd shared plans, imagining lives that would be lived with someone other than each other.

"Didn't you tell me that your granny said Forrest was adamant about the place where the portrait of Marissa should be hung?"

"Yes. Apparently, after the war, it was put in the exact same location. Forrest had left marks showing where it should be hung."

"Wonder why," Dermott mused.

"Wish I knew."

"Ready to look at the chandelier?"

Shaking her head to clear it of confusion, she slipped off her witch boots and headed for the table. "Help hoist me up. Maybe if we're lucky, I'll find real diamonds."

Placing both hands on the smooth polished wood, she realized the table, just like so many things in the house, emitted warmth, almost like a living thing. Or maybe all the warmth came from Dermott's palm, which she felt slide around the instep of her foot. Skin touched skin with almost kinetic force, then she experienced a moment's weightlessness before her knee landed on the tabletop. Standing on the table, she gazed down at him. Lamplight was dancing in his hair, touching the dark strands and making them appear almost golden, and he was staring up at her, shadows rippling across his stubbly jaw.

"If I check out the rest of the house, will you be okay?"

Nervously, she glanced from her own ring finger to the portrait again. Sure, Dermott believed there was a reasonable explanation, but she didn't. Magic was at work. "I'll be fine. Mug's here." Lowering her voice and turning in his direction, she crooned, "And you're a big bodyguard dog, aren't you, Muggy? A cute little bitty pit bull, right? No? Oh, sorry, Mug. You're a mean, nasty Doberman in a pug body."

Excited, Mug yipped, dropped his stick and began dutifully sniffing the baseboards for ghosts, as if to say he was ready to get down to business. She said, "Don't worry, Dermott. He'll protect me." As if to prove the point, the tiny dog glimpsed his own shadow, leaped in the air, whirled and attacked. Her shoulders shaking with merriment, Bridget said, "Go head. We'll be fine."

Dermott headed for the door. "I'll put away the groceries, then check upstairs. I could use some shut-eye soon."

"Me, too. It's early, but I'm beat. This will only take a couple of minutes. I'll shriek if I see any ghosts, I promise."

He chuckled again, the sound throaty. "That should give me time to run to the car."

"Oh, thanks," she said loftily. "My hero."

"I take that back," he amended. "Call if it's Lavinia. I know a few people who could use a voodoo-doll likeness."

But not a love potion? "I'll be sure to tell her." Her nose crinkled. "Unless I'm one of them. You have to admit, though," she added, "the smell of cigars is really strong in here. It's a little creepy."

"Hmm. What else was your dad known for?"

"Gambling hard. Riding horses. Fishing late at night."

"I'll bet you there's a bottle around here, and that it doesn't belong to him. When I find that whiskey, are you game for shooters?"

"That would warm me up. But I'll pass on smoking any cigars. Do you really think Granny Ginny's been drinking and smoking?"

"Of course. She's tracked mud into the house and left the door open, too." His eyes locked on hers, his lips twitching. "I just hope the whiskey's aged, the cigars are from Cuba and that he wears a size twelve, since my own shoes are soaked."

"I'll find the diamonds," Bridget said. "You find the booze."

"Deal."

Her breath caught as she watched him go. He had a great butt. There was no mistaking that. Even though they were just friends, this wasn't the first time she'd noticed that particular feature. When they walked around Greenwich Village, the predominantly gay neighborhood where they'd grown up and where her parents still lived, she always got a kick out of watching guys on Christopher Street checking out Dermott.

Turning to her task, she explored the chandelier, moving methodically. Pausing only to coo at Mug, who was just as carefully sniffing the floor, she traced each prism; they hung in clusters that reminded her of ripe grapes and were cool to the touch with ice-smooth edges and sharp contours. When they jingled, the soft sound made her think of antique music boxes, and she found herself wishing her boss at Tiffany's could see this, since he loved beautiful, sparkly things.

From where she stood, so close to the prisms, their color looked even bolder. The weak light emitted by the room's lamp hardly did it justice, Bridget knew, but with a fire in the fireplace and candles burning among the crystals, the fixture's multicolored rays would shine into all the dark corners. Her heart suddenly pulled, swelling inside her chest. It was a twisting pang she associated with fear of loss, the kind of pang she felt when she thought about failed love affairs, like Marissa and Forrest's, or when she couldn't remember exactly how the Trade Centers had looked. "What's wrong with me?" she whispered.

Why did she feel so sure she was going to lose Dermott? It was almost as if the ghosts of Hartley House had reached out just now and plucked at her heartstrings. Suddenly, she wished she was more like her sister, Marley, who was too cynical to be taken in deeply by the stories of the haunting. And while Edie was the consummate romantic, it was Bridget who'd always felt too much. She cried too easily, laughed too loudly and nothing more than ghost stories could send chills down her spine.

As soon as she'd heard Granny Ginny talking, she'd known she'd wind up coming here. And now she couldn't help but remember that her own father, her mom's first husband, had died…

…while standing on this very table.

Supposedly, he'd been very drunk when he'd taken the tumble that had cost his life. But what had he been doing up here? Looking at the prisms? Just as a shiver shook her shoulders, she could swear the pungent aroma of cigars filled the air once more. She started to call Dermott, but was calmed when she heard his footsteps above her. Besides...

"There's nobody with us, is there Mug?" she whispered, now anxious to finish. As she did, she couldn't help but feel a rush of disappointment. Each prism was achingly beautiful, but none hid clusters of diamonds. Suddenly, she startled. Blinking, she wondered how long she'd been here. It could have been moments or hours. She had a vague feeling that she'd lost time...maybe a lot of time. Hours. A day. A week. But that was crazy! Her eyes darted to the mantel clock. Shaped like a miniature grandfather clock, it was tall, with black Roman numerals on its face. The hands were stopped at midnight.

It was the exact hour Miss Marissa's marriage was to have taken place. Shaking her head to clear it of confusion, Bridget glanced at her wrist before realizing she wasn't wearing a watch. "Get a grip," she whispered. Hours couldn't have passed. Dermott would have come back downstairs by now, and yet she felt so inexplicably disoriented. She lifted her voice, fighting sudden panic. "Dermott?"

She waited what seemed an inordinately long time for his response, feeling glad when Mug trotted over, sat beneath the table and stared at her as she began to climb down.

His voice sounded from far away. "Everything okay, Bridge?"

"Fine," she called. "Where are you?"

"Upstairs, and uh, Bridge...you might want to come up."

What was wrong? "Coming!" Scooping Mug to her chest, she cast another glance around the room, her eyes lingering on the lifelike portrait of Miss Marissa and the ring. Too scared to turn off the lights, she moved quickly through the rooms she'd traversed earlier with Dermott. When she reached the shadowy, red-carpeted staircase, she stared up, glad to see a glimmer from what looked to be the nearest room to the top.

"No diamonds," she announced a moment later as she breezed across the threshold of a bedroom; it was more brightly decorated than any of the other rooms she'd seen. Rain was falling hard, pelting windows in which she could see her reflection. Lace curtains had been drawn back, and now, when lightning sizzled past, the world outside sparkled, briefly illuminated. She could see orange groves, and beyond them, swirling black waters.

"Sorry," said Dermott, who was crouched near a fireplace.

"About?"

"Scaring you."

She shrugged. "I didn't find the ring."

"Tomorrow," he promised.

Her voice caught. "I hope. I know it's here somewhere."

"I did find these." Turning on his haunches, he lifted a whiskey bottle and cigar stub, both of which were rimmed by bright pink lipstick, the same color favored by Granny Ginny.

So much for the idea that the scents came from the ghosts. "So, Granny does enjoy traditionally male pleasures," Bridget said, her anxiety ebbing since she was in a well-lit room with Dermott.

He said, "Care for a nightcap?"

"Sure," she said, taking in an impossibly high iron bed in the room's center; it was covered with a buttery yellow spread that matched sunshine walls and a lustrous glow from hardwood floors. An armoire was in one corner, and a dresser laid with an antique wash basin. Yes…in this welcoming room, the pinpricks she'd felt downstairs suddenly seemed ridiculous. Even though it was storming ferociously, the room was so bright it could have been a summer day. "It's lovely," she said, feeling delighted as Dermott handed her the whisky bottle and returned to the fire.

"Glad you like it," he returned, glancing over his shoulder as he placed a log across the andirons, stuffed a paper beneath it and lit it. "Because it's the only usable bedroom in the house."

Because that meant he'd have to sleep with her, she felt her pulse accelerate. Bands tightened around her chest, and all she could think was that this solved her problem. With him next to her, it would be easy to… Her hand tightened around the whiskey bottle, and she lifted it to her lips, downing a quick shot. She wasn't a big drinker, but she actually liked the taste, the slow burn wending down her throat.

"No one's been in the other rooms for years." He cracked a smile. "I'll put it this way, if your grandmother's really got ghosts, the other rooms are an open invitation."

"That bad?"

"Worse," he assured. "I'll sleep downstairs."

Oh, no, he wouldn't. "On those dusty sofas?" The air seemed suddenly charged, at least to her, and she could swear his eyebrows raised because he wanted to ask what she was suggesting. At the moment, however, she wasn't sure which motivated her more—her recent feelings of lust, or her fear of ghosts. Either way, she knocked back another nip of liquid courage and said, "Why don't you just sleep here with me?"

His eyes were unreadable. "In bed?"

Feeling her cheeks warming with the whiskey, she cast her eyes toward the hard wooden floor. She wanted to say any protest was ridiculous, since they'd camped out countless times before, and even shared beds, years ago, after college study marathons. But suddenly, for no reason at all, this felt so different. "Well, definitely not on the floor," she managed. "There's not even a rug…"

"Well, maybe for a night," he said, not sounding convinced.

"Tomorrow, we can air out one of the other rooms," she suggested, keeping her voice steady, even though the beat of her heart was anything but.

"Sounds like a plan."

The air seemed to crackle, and she was pretty sure they were both holding their breaths. It was the perfect time for a siren to whoop, sounding very close by. "The police," she said, grateful for the intrusion. Quickly, she set down the bottle and headed for the door before things could turn messy and awkward. Dermott was definitely going to be in her bed tonight, which meant she'd accomplished part of her plan. Once there, all she'd have to do was propose something more…

As she hurried downstairs, Dermott followed, moving so close behind her that she could smell his breath again. He, too, had apparently taken a swig of Granny Ginny's firewater. The scent fanned near her ear, sending tingles down her spine. By the time she opened the door, she was thinking about that big, empty bed again, and her knees were feeling impossibly weak. She stared at the tall, skinny, tan-uniformed black man on the porch.

"Zechariah Walsh," he boomed, charging across the threshold, a hand resting—and not casually—on his gun holster, the snap to which was open. "I went up to Nancy's Diner for dinner, and everybody told me you two were here, then the dispatcher called," he announced, peering between them with sharp dark eyes that had seen too much of the world. "But I didn't believe it. No, sir. That Ginny Hartley is the most self-centered woman! Sending young people such as yourselves in here, unprepared."

Shaking his head, he quickly continued, "So, they left the front door open, did they? Who'd you see first? Lavinia or Jasper? Those two need to be read the riot act! Even when he was living, Jasper Lee, that was his middle name and what folks around here called him, you know…well, he could raise more hell than any fire-and-brimstone sermon you'd hear in a Baptist hall." Pausing, he blew out a sigh. "I don't know what you two expect me to do, though. Handcuffs don't hold this bunch. Ginny had me try that once, but metal goes right through 'em."

Bridget's lips had parted in surprise, and now she glanced over her shoulder at Dermott whose mouth was curling at the corners. "Excuse me, Sheriff Walsh," she managed.

"Marissa or Forrest?" he demanded, not heeding her. Putting his hands on his hips, the sheriff was clearly starting to lose his patience. "Is that who's causing such a stir?" Suddenly, his eyes narrowed to tiny dark pinpoints, and he pursed his lips tightly before suddenly exploding, "Oh, I get it! Yes, sir, I get the picture now. Didn't your Granny Ginny even bother to warn you that her place is haunted?"

3

"THAT SHERIFF'S as crazy as one of your old boy-friends," Dermott murmured with a soft chuckle an hour later, whispering over the soft patter of rain that came in the wake of the storm; they were lying in bed in the dark.

"I can't believe he—and everybody else around here—really believes this place is haunted," Bridget whispered shakily.

"Scared?"

"Yeah," she admitted. "Are you? Is that why you're still awake? I thought you were ready to conk out."

"The ghosts," he lied. "That's it." His sleeplessness had nothing to do with lying next to Bridget, who was nearly naked, he tried to tell himself. Still, he was so wide-awake that someone could have injected him with adrenaline. The whole time he and Sheriff Walsh had rechecked the doors and windows, he'd had his mind on only one thing—whether he was going to get into bed with Bridget. Oh, he knew what she was thinking. They'd shared sleeping quarters on camping trips and during study marathons; when she was depressed over breakups, they'd cuddled in a way that could even be called suggestive.

But he needed a bed. He was bone tired from driving, annoyed with Carrie's constant phone calls, and the sofas were dusty, the floor too hard. On the other hand, this was a soft feather bed in an old-fashioned room designed for romance, and as he squinted into the darkness, he listened to the romantic sounds of rain and the last cracklings of the fire. Burning cedar edged out the pungent aroma of cigar smoke, making room for Bridget's perfume. It didn't help that they'd knocked back a few shots after Sheriff Walsh had gone, either, which meant liquor was curling in his gut, fanning downward, leaving his groin taut. Uttering a soft sound of frustration, he stroked Mug, who'd curled into the crook of his arm.

Bridget whispered, "We could only wish all my dates had been apparitions."

"I liked Antonio," Dermott teased, stretching his legs, enjoying the luxurious feel of his own muscles. "He was definitely flesh and blood. Which is why we found out he had a wife in Mexico."

"Duane was more sincere," agreed Bridget.

Duane had joined the Moonies, then tried to convert Bridget. "Selling flowers in airports wasn't the right career for you."

His shoulders lifted with a dry chuckle. "Remember that guy who shaved his whole body? He kept asking me if I'd ever shaved…"

"Your privates. Right."

She paused. "And Arthur. I haven't thought about him in years. Remember? The obsessive guy from Queens who kept serenading me?"

"With seventies songs. The eighties I could have

handled, but when I heard Sonny and Cher's 'I Got You Babe'..."

"You called the cops."

"What else could I do, Bridge? You'd even started dressing like him, wearing beads, bell-bottoms and tie-dyed shirts. You looked like you were auditioning for a part in a Richard Linklater movie."

She considered. "Hmm. Well...we could sure use Marco now."

Marco had done magic tricks for kids' birthday parties.

"To make the ghosts vanish?"

"It's what he did to me."

Literally. During a party, Marco had put Bridget in a box, tapped it with a wand and promptly forgotten her until she'd found him naked in bed with a birthday boy's mother two hours later. Catching a whiff of the floral scent wafting from Bridget's skin, Dermott suddenly wished he'd slept on a sofa, after all. Respiratory failure from dust might have been preferable to how his emotions were twisting into knots. Carrie had called his cell while he'd been exploring upstairs, subtly pressuring him to get back to New York, the implication being that she'd be waiting for him—wet and wild—in bed. He'd gotten defensive, arguing that he and Bridget had just arrived, which was true, and Carrie had zeroed right in on the change in his mood.

She was right, too. Instead of extricating himself, he was getting drawn into Bridget's world again— enjoying her whimsical clothes, visionary ideas and the warm feelings he experienced when he watched her pamper Mug. He liked the low-maintenance, easy banter they shared, and how they could drive for hours in a silence born out of knowing each other for years. To some, Bridget might seem flighty, mostly because of her constant chatter about clothes, movies, books and lifestyle trends, but he'd always found a hunger for life that matched his own, and an affinity for culture and beauty that was the stuff of their respective arts. His thoughts turned to the upcoming project he was doing in L.A. right before Allison and Kenneth's wedding, and his heart wrenched. By then, would he have done what he'd told Carrie he'd come to do?

"Dermott," Bridget suddenly whispered. "I could swear I left the downstairs lights on when I came up."

He tried to sound sleepier than he really was, and he wished he was already in L.A. It was easy to immerse himself in work in the studio. Right now, that seemed the only time he'd really forgotten Bridget, at least for a few moments. "The lights," he echoed, jogging his own mind. "So?"

"So, when Sheriff Walsh got here, they were off."

"Probably you turned them off and forgot."

"No. I'm sure." She paused, her voice catching with apprehension. "It's so quiet here…isn't it?"

"Just go to sleep."

"But it *is* too quiet," she insisted.

Telling himself to try to sleep, he wound up rolling to his side instead and propping himself on an elbow. "Don't get creeped out, Bridge. Just listen. The night's full of sounds," he coached, his voice husky with whiskey. "And none of them come from ghosts."

In the next second, he could hear the crick in her neck and the brushing rustle of fabric as she turned her head on the pillow to do as he suggested. The patter of rain had nearly stopped, but stray drops fell from gutters, splashing onto soft, wet leaves. Nearer, the fire's last embers crackled. From far off, he could swear he heard soft plunks of water in the swamp as lizards, fish and alligators went about nocturnal routines. Even the shadowy clouds visible through the curtains seemed to carry sounds—thundering piano music, crashing cymbals, drum rolls. Bridget's face seemed to communicate sounds to him, too. He took in the slits of eyes, ski-jump nose and upturned lips.

Even as he silently cursed himself for noticing, he couldn't help but wish things had been different, that they'd become lovers in the past. After all, this was the kind of experience lovers shared. "If I was writing the sound track," he couldn't help but murmur, "I'd use something dark and heavy. Maybe Wagner."

"Don't forget to throw in some howls of werewolves." She paused. "Edie wants you to do the music for Julia Darden's wedding. Julia's picked out some songs, but nothing seems to really work for her. Edie thought you might help with some input, maybe even suggest alternative musicians. She told me that you already said no, but I'm supposed to talk you into it over the next few days."

"Nice segue." He could hardly tell Bridget he'd said no because he was trying to distance himself from her. "I don't do weddings."

"It's not just any wedding," she corrected, yawning. "It's high-profile. It'll get you mentions in mags."

Again, he felt a strong tug on his emotions; it was as if the undercurrent of the tidewaters in the swamp were inside him, sucking him deeper into Bridget's world—her dreams, needs, desires. "I...have too much other work to do. As soon as we get back, I'm going to L.A. for a long weekend, remember?"

"Which means you can think on the plane. Anyway, Edie can wait another week for your real answer." She flashed him a smile. "At least until Allison and Kenneth's wedding." Yawning, she added, "I'm determined to make you change your mind."

"I won't."

Not sounding perturbed, she whispered, "We should have brought in the sound equipment from the car."

"You really think we'll hear ghosts tonight?"

"Zechariah Walsh thought so."

"I'll bring in the recorders tomorrow," he promised, still studying the shadowy outline of her face. "I'm too tired to set them up now." Even though she was tucked under the covers, and he'd elected to stay on top, he knew she was wearing hip-hugger sweatpants and a midriff with spaghetti straps under which she was braless. While there was no mistaking Carrie Masterson's implants, Bridget was the real deal. Her breasts curved at the exact same angle as her ski-jump nose, and just thinking about her nipples beneath the paper-thin cotton took away his breath. She rolled on the feather mattress, burrowing her face in a pillow. If he didn't know better, he'd think she was tossing and turning because of his proximity.

"Is Mug bothering you?" she asked.

"He's okay. Just go to sleep, Bridge."

He felt the warmth leave his side as Mug got up and trotted to Bridget. Lifting an edge of the covers by nudging it with his head, the pup flattened his body and crawled beneath. With her eyes half-shut, Bridget shifted her weight as the dog snuggled next to her. "I think he's scared, too, Dermott."

"That, or he got an upset stomach after he ate our leftovers from that greasy spoon next to the Bates Motel."

She laughed. "They'd never seen the likes of us, pardner."

"You tried grits and gravy," he commended. "Very brave for a New Yorker."

"Wait until you see me battle Lavinia's ghost." Quickly, she added, "Did you hear that?"

"What?"

She chuckled. "The ghosts."

She'd only been teasing him. "No." But it was a lie. He heard them everywhere, in the thundering clouds and the poof of feathers when she moved on the bed. Flashes of memory kept claiming him—how she'd talked him into buying his apartment in Battery Park City, or how her face lit up when she played with his sister's kids, or how beautiful Viv Benning's decorations looked at Christmas. Suddenly, his heart ached. "Go to sleep, Bridge. We've got a big day tomorrow. We'll vanquish the ghosts, then move on to your diamond hunt."

"I can't believe the ring wasn't in the chandelier."

He was sorry she was disappointed. "We'll find

it," he promised, even though they both knew it was probably a lie. Still, if they did, maybe he could slip the ring—the real ring—onto her finger, end the curse and get her married off. In a week, he'd be back in New York, making love to Carrie Masterson, who was warm, willing and waiting.

Her voice was faint, sounding so far off that he imagined they'd moved on to separate lives, and she was already a world away. "'Night, Dermott."

His throat felt strangely tight, and when he spoke, the words were a croak. "See you in the morning," he said. And then, as he listened to the haunting night sounds, he heard the exact moment her breath evened, and he knew she'd fallen asleep.

HER FEVERISH SKIN burned, and, feeling panicked, Bridget tried to calm her pounding heart and racing blood, but how could she? Bullets were flying across the rain-swept night in red arcs of fire that looked like scars. Hooves thundered, plowing up clods of wet earth. Someone called, "Marissa? Where are you? Hurry!"

But she had to hide the ring! Casting her eyes wildly around the room, she scanned the parlor, twisting the Hartley diamond on her finger. She took in the glittering prisms. Some were as big as the diamond and just as sparkly…but no. She and Lavinia hadn't been able to take down the chandelier, but Union soldiers might do so.

"Hurry, Miss Marissa! We haven't much time!"

Her pulse leaped in her throat. Where could she put the ring? Why hadn't she listened to Lavinia, and let her hide it underneath the floorboards upstairs? Her eyes searched the round rug edged in fringe, then the floorboards, the jagged stones of the fireplace and heavy curtains. "I'll put it in our special place," she whispered.

And then the dream shifted, and she was outside, racing now, running toward the swamp to hide. *Where is my lover?* she thought, her heart bursting in pain as she plunged through the rain. *My dress,* she thought in horrified stupor. The gorgeous white gown hand-sewn by her and her sisters was ruined, its lovely fabric streaked with mud. She lifted her skirts high—her neck craning, her eyes scanning the trees for Forrest. Tonight, he was going to marry her, to make love with her in the big iron bed upstairs...

She scooted closer and closer, almost into her lover's arms, even as the dream fractured, breaking into nonsensical fragments. She was naked now, and as she moved nearer, her skin turned fiery hot. Slightly lifting her leg, she glided it alongside his, exploring the contours of his feet with her own, his calves, the bunched muscles of his thighs. And then, under the cover of the midnight darkness, his mouth covered hers—hot, wet, wild—his tongue thrusting hard, until the dream shifted again.

Now she was running once more—madly running for her life—into the dark, dank waters of the swamp. Lavinia was up ahead, her hair in cornrows and tied with a kerchief. "Here, child," she said, and then the damp chilled her as she sank into it, moss and slime rising around her beautiful wedding dress. She was scared...so very scared! Would this nightmare never end? Her eyes scanned the liquid sky as wind whipped her gaze. Her heart lurched, and then she saw him! But it wasn't Forrest at all...

No. She wasn't Marissa now, was she? It was the present, she was Bridget Benning again, and her lover was Dermott Brandt...

"HURRY!" A hand was shaking her shoulder, shaking her, and the voice was hushed and urgent. Was it Forrest? "We've got to get out of here!" She must still be dreaming, she thought, and then she coughed, intaking a breath. "Cigars," she muttered. Were the ghosts here? Was she about to see the ghost of her biological father, a man she didn't even remember, burning tobacco as her Granny Ginny claimed could happen?

And what had happened to her plans for the night? She'd been so determined to seduce Dermott, but she'd lost her nerve. He'd seemed too distant, somehow, and she sensed it wasn't the right time. Her throat felt tight; she was choking. Blinking in the darkness, her eyes stung. "Were you smoking?"

"No, Bridge. C'mon. You've got to get up."

She struggled to consciousness, the smell thick and overwhelming. Her eyes stung as her lungs sucked in air. "The fire," she managed to say, feeling unnaturally groggy as she pushed away the covers. Dermott was already out of bed. Alarmed, she swung her legs over the side, and rose, a shiver rippling through her as she felt the smooth slide of sweatpant fabric— his and hers—and then...yes. Unmistakably an erection. Heat followed in the wake of the shiver-ripples.

"Are you awake now, Bridge?"

Oh, yes. Narrowing her eyes and looking around, she tried to get her bearings. "There's somebody outside," she whispered hoarsely, unable to see beyond curtains that Dermott had closed, but sensing movement. Rapidly blinking, she realized the fire had gone out. The smoke was from elsewhere. The room was as dark as pitch, and cold.

"Do you feel a draft?" she croaked.

"Yeah. C'mon. Let's get our stuff."

"What do you mean—get our stuff?"

As he darted toward the door, she realized the house had come alive with sounds. Mug was still in bed, whimpering, and she could swear she heard footsteps in the hallway. "Do you hear that?" Voices floated up the staircase. Had Sheriff Walsh come back? Even though she couldn't make out the words, the urgent cadence of the voices reminded her of her dream.

Scooping up Mug, so his paws hooked over her shoulders, she edged out of bed, squealing since the wood beneath her feet felt frozen. Seeing that Dermott had reversed directions, she headed toward the window, shivering when she reached his side. "I felt a draft," she whispered. "I know I did. It was really cold. I think it was coming from under the bed." Thinking of horror movies she'd seen, she blew out a breath, but it was too dark to see if her breath fogged the air.

"I felt it, too," Dermott whispered.

"What's going on?"

"I don't know—" Dermott pulled back the lace curtain "—but look at this."

Her jaw slackened as she took in what looked like a laser show. Red trajectories of fire arched between trees, then traced squiggles in the night air. Explosions of red, blue and yellow shot closer to the ground, looking like rifle fire. From far off, she heard thunder, and she thought it was still storming, but then she realized no rain was falling. "Horses," she said, the word barely audible.

"Coming down the shell road," he murmured.

Her heart hammered dangerously hard, and she jumped, bumping Dermott who quickly wrapped an arm around her. "What's that?"

She barely heard him answer. "I don't know."

Past the orange groves, near the swamp, watery colors seemed to rise in the darkness, trailing from the ground whimsically like the smoke from one of Jasper's cigars. Attempting to ignore the sounds, she continued to try to rationalize what was happening as she peered at the swimming colors…white, blue, red, yellow. This couldn't be happening, she thought, and yet something completely supernatural seemed to be unfolding before her eyes.

She watched in stupefied terror as the white color congealed like morning mist in the black night, turning more solid and less transparent as it took shape, looking like a bell, then an hourglass…

"A skirt! It's Marissa's wedding dress!" Beside the materializing white form, other colors wove into the darkness like threads on a loom, with a yellow warp thread and a blue woof, forming another skirt. A face floated above, but it was hard to discern the features, since her skin showed darkness upon darkness.

"Lavinia?" It was still too dark to tell, but Bridget's heart jump-started when the swimming colors that looked like dresses began floating from the swamp, toward the house. The nearer they came, the more they took form, and she knew she'd never been so glad to feel Dermott's arm around her shoulders...

"That's it," Dermott said succinctly. "Let's go. Now."

Half-paralyzed, torn between wanting to see and wanting to run, Bridget edged away from the window as the women's faces became sharper, more distinct. As if drawn from gray fog, an outline of a white oval appeared, arches of dark eyebrows, the dot of a red mouth. Lavinia was shadier, but discernable now, lighter than the night, her hair wrapped in a kerchief.

"This is rigged," Dermott whispered.

She tried to believe it. "Maybe someone's trying to scare Granny Ginny. There could be some sort of projector in the trees."

"Yeah," he said, not sounding convinced. "And a sound system."

As his hand settled on her lower back, her spinal fluid turned to ice. The women looked too real. Gooseflesh stippled her back as she watched them continue floating toward the house, and the tips of her breasts peaked as if she'd been dunked in ice water.

"Hurry, Miss Marissa!" came a voice. Or at least Bridget *thought* she heard a voice. Maybe she was going crazy. Or still dreaming. But Dermott was awake, too. Was this some form of shared hallucination? Granny had filled her mind with stories for years, and now...

She turned toward Dermott. "Where's my coat?"

"Downstairs. Hung over the banister."

She could grab it on the way out. "Yours?"

"Same place."

Swiftly turning, she muttered, "What if they suddenly speed up?" She thought of countless horror movies where ghost figures raced forward, still as statues, their motion rocketlike. Dermott had reached the door. Quickly grabbing their bags, he said, "Let's try to make the SUV before those things reach the house."

Those things. Who knew what they really were? If they weren't part of a ruse, projections from hidden cameras, then…

Suddenly, meeting Marissa and Lavinia at the door didn't seem like a particularly good idea. After all, it was their house, right? Maybe they didn't want company. Speeding her steps, Bridget ran behind Dermott, shoving her feet into her witch boots.

Dermott hit a switch. "No lights, Bridge."

Heavy footsteps sounded in the hallway as she and Dermott fled downstairs. The steps shuffled, brushing the wood floor, then the person seemed to stagger. Choking on her own fear, Bridget clutched Mug so tight he yelped. He was shivering now, shaking in her arms. She was muttering encouragements she didn't really feel when Dermott whisked her cape around her shoulders.

Already, she thought what she'd seen upstairs had to have been her imagination. As Dermott opened the front door, the blast of night air gusted through her bones. She paused on the wraparound porch, hearing Dermott slam the door, then he grabbed her free hand.

"The horses!" she gasped.

Hooves thundered toward them on the shell road, and time accelerated as they ran toward the SUV. Flexing her fingers, she held Dermott's tight. Relief flooded her at the touch—the living warmth of his flesh, the response as his fingers curled around hers. Her pulse pounding, she let go of his hand, letting him run to the driver's side. Surges of adrenaline seemed to carry her, shooting through her veins like bullets as she lunged inside with Mug and slammed the door.

Simultaneously, they locked their doors, not that locks would deter ghosts, according to Zechariah Walsh. As Dermott turned the key in the ignition, the motor roared. Tires spun, spewing shells, and she gasped as they headed toward the main road, branches from the dark overhang of trees scraping the roof, pointing at the windshield like witches' fingers.

"Look, Dermott!"

Watery horses, mounted by Union soldiers, charged toward them at a brisk gallop, their heads down and mouths lathering. There were ten, maybe fifteen. Like holograms, they faded and reappeared, and she could see straight through them, into the trees beyond. "Are you going to drive through them?" she managed, her heart beating a fast tattoo when she saw one soldier bend, reaching for his sword.

"Looks like it."

She held her breath, bracing for impact that never came, then gasped in as the headlights pierced through horses and riders; they charged through the car, driving through the night, unstopping. And then they were past.

Glancing over her shoulder, through the back windows, she ogled the backs of the horses, their muscled buttocks flinching, their tails flying. Most went ahead, but one rider stayed behind, and just as he drew his sword, she inhaled sharply, sensing what was to come. She watched, her heart lurching, her mouth forming a warning as a blade arced. "Forrest," she murmured as a man stepped from the trees…

Then she saw nothing. Only darkness until, through an upstairs window, a light snapped on. Shadows moved behind a curtain. Dermott stepped on the gas pedal, and a moment later, when Bridget turned back around, the window was lost to sight. Had they really just witnessed something paranormal? "Where are we going?" she managed, knowing that the town of Big Swamp was only two blocks long.

"We don't have much choice," Dermott said, wrenching the steering wheel hard as they turned onto the main road. "Back to the diner and the motel."

"Great," she whispered, glad once more that she was sharing this adventure with Dermott. "We're going to the Bates Motel?"

4

As soon as Bridget dropped Mug onto a dark shag carpet in the motel, he shivered, raced into the bathroom and curled up next to a heater. Bridget knelt, her shoulders shaking from fear and the night air, her eyes wide with questions about what she'd just seen as she rifled through her duffel and withdrew a doggie T-shirt on which was printed, "9-11 Firedog." Quickly, she slipped Mug's quivering paws into the sleeves, then returned to the main room where Dermott was fiddling with the heater system. As he pressed a button, the radiator rattled to life.

Her voice quivering, Bridget said, "Can you believe they kept a room ready for us here?"

"Trés creepy," he agreed. The woman at the front desk had said she'd heard about their visit from Sheriff Walsh, and because the haunting at Hartley House had worsened over time, the proprietress had kept a room open, since she was sure they wouldn't make it through the night. Earlier today, Dermott would have laughed. Now, he felt uneasy.

Bridget glanced around. "This place really does look like the Bates Motel in *Psycho.*"

"It's…" As Dermott searched for a word, he recalled how eerie the mist had looked, rising from phosphorescent swamp grass, and how smoky red air had magically materialized into the floating women. "*Safer*," he finished decisively, dragging splayed fingers through his hair, scarcely seeing the double bed, which was covered by a frayed spread and equipped with a quarter slot. A television rested on a scarred dresser that was carved with initials. Despite the ragtag furniture, he was glad they were at the motel. Had they been in real danger? "Your grandmother's place must be rigged with projectors and sound equipment," he ventured, his eyes searching hers. "It's got to be."

Bridget hugged her arms to her waist. "Oh, I don't know, Dermott," she managed, her voice quivering slightly, as if the alternative was simply too much to contemplate. "I believe in ghosts. I admit it. My grandmother's been telling me those stories for years. But maybe you're right." She paused, and despite the wary look in her eyes, her voice hitched with excitement. "If you're not, though, maybe everything else Granny said is true, and when I do find the ring, the curse will end."

Be that as it may, Dermott wanted to find a reasonable explanation. "Didn't you say your grandmother was having trouble?"

"She does have enemies," Bridget admitted with a shiver. "She said her neighbor, Mavis Benchley, can't stand her. The families have been feuding since the war." Casting a glance toward the bathroom to check on Mug, Bridget unbuttoned the cape and shrugged out of the garment, baring the midriff and hip-hugging sweats. "As the story goes on, the Benchleys hid on their property the night the Yankees came and didn't ask Marissa and Lavinia to join them."

"And they died because of it," Dermott murmured. Things rarely bothered him, but every time he recalled those women materializing, as if out of the fog, his blood ran cold.

"Granny Ginny mentioned a pawnbroker in town, too, Garth Cousins. She said he's been trying to buy her land for years, but there was something in the way she spoke about him…"

"Something?"

"Odd. Like she wasn't telling me the whole story."

"Maybe Mavis or Garth did something to the property." His voice trailed off, since he couldn't imagine how such realistic ghosts could have been produced by an elderly neighbor or a local pawnbroker.

"To make it look as if the place is haunted?"

"I don't know," he mused, rubbing his hands together. "A production like that would take a lot of equipment." Was it his imagination? Or had the hems of the dresses blown in exact tandem with the breeze, moving with the leaves of the trees. A camera couldn't have done that.

"At first I believed the stories might be true," she quickly said. "But now…"

She'd seen evidence, and, like him, she was trying to refute it. "There are no such things as ghosts, Bridge," he assured. "That's not what I'm suggesting."

She hesitated. "Uh…you're not?"

He shook his head. Working on movies had taught him that reality was a mere chimera. In the hands of a master, it could be easily manipulated, twisted into unrecognizable forms. Even the most skeptical viewer could be made to believe anything. He recalled the straining necks of the horses, their taut muscles, their short, bristly hairs sleek with sweat. Red streaks of fire had stretched like burning fingers of flame into the sky, and the white puffs of smoke on the lawn had looked authentic, as if they'd come from muskets. What they'd seen was too complex for a person to stage without expertise, but it could be done.

"I didn't see anyone on the property, did you?"

She shook her head. "No. Just…" *Those things.*

He sighed, thinking out loud. "Given the size of the light display, someone would have to be working the controls."

She nodded sagely. "The man behind the curtain."

"Or woman."

He'd been eyeing her as he voiced his thoughts, and now Dermott noted how the night air had affected her, turning her cheeks pink and enlivening her blue eyes. Then he thought again of the watery colors materializing near the swamp, solidifying until Marissa's white, porcelain-smooth face was clear. He'd seen hints of Lavinia's dark features, flashes of her teeth and the whites of her eyes, and when they'd reached the road, the horses had been impressive, looming from the shadows, the lawn's massive trees visible through transparent bodies. They'd been running hard, champing at the bit.

"There was something odd about the sound," he suddenly murmured, shutting his eyes, replaying the thundering hooves, and then the rocket fire. He heard clods of dirt flying, a soft high whinny, then a neigh. Yes, something about the sound niggled. It reminded him of…

"What?"

Shaking his head to clear it of confusion, he said, "I don't know, Bridge." But something from his subconscious was trying to surface. Pushing aside the thought, he found himself saying, "You look like you came from an amusement park, not a haunted house."

Concern was still in her eyes, but they were dancing, too, in a way that made his breath catch. "There were certainly some similarities, don't you think?"

"A real thrill ride." Right now, her eyes reminded him of the intricately cut prisms in the parlor's chandelier; they sparkled so much they could have been chiseled by a master hand.

She shook her head. "I don't know what I imagined would happen when we got here, but…"

"Not those fireworks?"

"It was crazy out there."

"If no one was working controls, then there has to be a remote system, maybe timers, Bridge. Maybe even a central sound system."

"Wouldn't equipment like that be damaged in this weather? It was raining pretty hard, Dermott. And why would anyone go to such trouble to create the impression that the place is haunted?"

"To scare your grandmother off her property. Wasn't that what you were suggesting?"

"It's a possibility. But why?"

"I don't know." His mind was still on another track. "Maybe the controls are inside the house. It didn't look as though your grandmother's been in some of the rooms for years, so if someone did want to make her house seem haunted, I don't think she'd have noticed anyone on the premises."

"No wonder she's scared and wants to stay in New York right now. When I saw Marissa and Lavinia, I thought I was going to have a heart attack. Didn't you?"

That made him smile. "How could I? I had to protect you."

Gratitude flashed in her eyes. Despite the twinge of irony, she wasn't joking when she said, "My hero."

The words made something catch in his throat, and that age-old wistful feeling he always got around Bridget Benning twisted inside his chest. Before he thought it through, he considered her a long moment and said, "Am I?"

"Who else?"

This was the kind of moment that had plagued him over the years, and he'd been trying hard not to set himself up for it. He had a sudden, wild impulse to cross the room, grab her, haul her against him, and say, "Damn you, Bridge. I told Carrie Masterson I wouldn't see you anymore, not even as friends, but I see the way you look at me sometimes. Why can't you face it? You've wanted it. I've wanted it." He shrugged and said instead, "One of your boyfriends."

"Yeah, right," she muttered dryly.

He could tell what they'd just been through had gotten to her. Her face was wan, her eyes uncertain, her smile teetering, as if it might crumble into a frown.

Wild from their run, her disheveled hair had come loose, and it was falling in thick hanks, fanning her face and tumbling over her bare shoulders. The rest of her body took away his breath, and even as he was damning himself for the unwanted response, she was also making him ache deliciously. Just as he forced himself to take a deep breath, his cell rang, and he glanced down to where it was attached to his belt, saw Carrie's number in the call window, and made the snap decision to flick the phone off, telling himself he'd call her later. Bridget made a point of not noticing. "If one of your grandmother's enemies is trying to run her off the property, what's the motive?"

She shrugged. "Spite. Or maybe timber. She said she's gotten a lot of offers. It's a fairly large acreage, thick with hardwood trees." Pausing, she considered. "Or maybe there's some other motive I haven't considered yet."

His eyes dropped from her face to the sweet, upturned curve of breasts visible beneath a scrap of dark blue cloth that matched her eyes. He wasn't particularly surprised to find himself getting aroused. He'd seen her so many ways—excited, amused, furious. Now he'd even seen her running from ghosts. But he'd never see her riding high on the brink of an orgasm. Her pants hung so low on her slender hips that one tug of a drawstring would send them down her long legs, and since he didn't see panty lines, he had to wonder what, if anything, she was wearing beneath. *Caught,* he realized. She'd been watching him check her out. Her eyes looked curious, too. As if she was wondering if he'd go for it. And yet he knew he had to be wrong about that. She'd rebuffed him in the past. Every time he'd tried to initiate a conversation about their attraction, he'd hit a brick wall.

Ghosts, he thought on a sigh. Every moment with Bridget was pregnant with years of recollections. It always felt like pieces of her had imprinted his brain on a cellular level and were never going to get dislodged. Just like the chandelier at Hartley House, her presence had taken up residence inside him and decided never to leave. But she was no ghost. She was flesh and blood. Nearly undressed and right in front of him. His chest constricted, and he forced himself to unhook the phone from his belt. "Despite all the excitement, I guess I'd better call Carrie back."

Bridget's expression was unreadable, and it was the wrong time to notice she'd gotten a sudden chill, and that the tips of her breasts had beaded, tightening against the flimsy cloth of her shirt…the wrong time to notice they were about to share another bed. She said, "We can look around the property tomorrow when it's light. See what we can find." She sighed. "Granny Ginny did say things have gotten worse over time."

"And they got worse after…" He paused a second, never really certain whether to call Jasper her father. It was true biologically, but she'd never known him. "After Jasper died."

Bridget nodded, still looking as if she simply couldn't believe any of this, something he understood since he shared the feelings. "She said Lavinia and Marissa always haunted the place, but not often."

"Did your mother ever see them? I mean, she lived in the house when she was married to Jasper, right?"

"Even if she had, Mom would never admit it," Bridget explained. "She'd feel she was lending credence to the wedding curse, and she doesn't want me or my sisters to believe in it. She thinks Granny screwed us up by putting all those family stories into our minds."

Dermott agreed with Viv. Had Bridget not been convinced she was cursed, her dating life might have run a lot more smoothly, in his opinion, so he settled for a noncommital "Hmm."

"According to Granny, things got worse after her son died, and by then, Mom had taken us back to New York." Stifling a yawn, she glanced toward the bed, making him sorry there was only one, but everyone in town, including the proprietress, kept assuming they were married, and this was the only available room.

Bridget seemed to read his mind. "Obviously, if you're having an affair in Big Swamp, you come here to…*you know.*"

He knew, all right. Every time he looked at Bridget he was thinking about…*you know.* "The place is definitely hopping," he agreed. Every parking space had been taken.

"Well, we should try to sleep. We can talk about it more in the morning. Are you tired?"

"A little." Less so when he watched her cross the room braless, her breasts bouncing under the nothing-shirt. When she leaned to turn down the double bed, he glimpsed cleavage, almost a nipple, and he abruptly turned away, deciding he should claim the armchair and just watch the tube until she fell asleep. "I think I'll watch some TV."

"You said you need to call Carrie back," she reminded, flicking on a bedside lamp. "Can you hit the overhead?"

He moved toward the light switch near the door, flipped it, then turned around—only to find she'd silently circled the bed and was coming straight toward him in the dimly illuminated room. The vision blindsided him. His chest constricted and the back of his throat went dry as his eyes took in scantily covered breasts, a bare belly and the rounded contours of her hips. His groin tightened painfully with a tug of longing he didn't want to deny. Silence surrounded them as if they were in a vacuum. Electricity filled the air. Vibrating and thrumming, its static charged him, making the hairs on his arms bristle. With the chin of her heart-shaped face tilted downward, he now realized she was peering at him from under heavy lids.

"What?" he murmured, vaguely wondering what was going on.

And then Bridget simply stepped forward. Her pelvis brushed where his groin was so achingly tight, and she wreathed her arms around his neck, pulling him to her. The moment felt so right, so unrehearsed, so real. The embrace was completely unexpected and yet he should have guessed...

Her hands glided, stroking the skin of his neck. Before he could think better of it, his arms responded, circling her waist, his blood quickening as his palms swept across her smooth bare back, registering the silken texture and heat.

"Are you okay?" he managed to say. "Scared?"

Her voice was promising, husky and nervous. "After what we just saw? Of course. But that's not why…I mean, I was just thinking…"

Thinking was dangerous, he decided as she dropped a long blue fingernail onto his chest. As she drew a circle on his shirt, his heart pounded like crazy beneath. *Very dangerous.* "Bridge," he ventured. "You're acting…funny."

"Funny?"

She knew what he was talking about. "Did the ghosts…"

"Put me under a spell?"

Now that she'd spoken the thought aloud, it sounded unlikely, but then, the whole evening had been strange. "Uh…yeah."

She smiled sleepily. "A sex spell."

Sex? Dammit, if he knew what was good for him, he'd back away right now and run in the other direction, or at least head for the privacy of the bathroom and call Carrie back. Traces of the whiskey they'd shared were on her breath, and her eyes had turned a shade darker, shifting from cerulean waters to mists at midnight. His voice hardened, and he inched backward. "You've had too much to drink."

"Maybe," she mused.

He backed away another inch.

And that's when she stretched on her tiptoes— seemingly to kiss him—then teetered and lost her balance. His arms caught her, tightening around her waist. Nothing romantic happened, not really. Her mouth slammed inelegantly against his shoulder, but that didn't stop those lips from burning right through his shirt. Groins didn't lock like puzzle pieces, but the curved bone of her pelvis repositioned, so a mound cushioned by impossibly soft hair pressed hard against an erection he wished he didn't have. But he did. It angled straight up against his belly, and his breath caught audibly when her breasts, so free beneath the tiny top, swept his chest, the taut nipples pebbling. Suddenly, he felt he had to feel them on his skin—her nipples against his, the slick heat of her body accepting his aroused length.

He tried to pull away once more, but her hands held him spellbound, cupping his face, her nails trailing a slow line down his cheek, and when she rose on her toes again, the sudden sweet touch of her mouth utterly did him in. The kiss, just like the embrace, came from nowhere, and yet he knew their whole lives had led to it.

His senses soared. The kiss was nothing more than the slow perfect pressure of warm, unadorned lips. They tasted of mint at first, with a hard lick of whiskey that came from behind. If she hadn't drawn away and glanced into his eyes for his reaction, he would have been a goner. But her hesitation brought him to his senses, bringing anger that was every bit as undeniable as his unmistakable hard-on. Damn it. After all these years, and after all the times he'd tried to proposition her, did she really think she could simply come on to him like this—and he'd just roll over? What did she think he was—her dog? "What's this about, Bridge?"

"I want to sleep with you."

Words were forming before he thought them through, and if the truth be told, he'd waited just as many years to speak them as he'd waited to have her beneath him in bed. "You're not going to play with my emotions, Bridge. Not now. Not at this stage of the game."

She looked crushed, her face falling. "Game?" she managed to say. "Stage? What are you talking about?"

She knew. She was a few inches shorter than he, so he was staring down into her eyes, and while he knew it was a mistake, knew he had to get farther away from her, he felt paralyzed.

"It's just sex," she urged.

He couldn't believe how hot she looked for it, either, as she offered the half raise of a bare shoulder that looked so shiny, smooth and winter-pale that his mouth watered. "Aren't you curious?"

That was the problem. He had been for years. He'd dropped plenty of hints about them winding up in bed, not to mention forced a few overt conversations. Now he tried to look unaffected, even though she'd had to have realized he was painfully aroused. "You're the one who's always said no."

"That was then."

He leaned closer, then wished he hadn't. Her breath was on his cheek, his lips and in his hair. "Why now?" he demanded softly.

When she swallowed hard, looking rejected, he was surprised to find that he didn't really care. For so many years, he'd fantasized about this moment.

They'd be alone somewhere. Standing under dim light. A thousand times he'd imagined her lifting a shirt over her head, pulling down her slacks, or stepping out of a slip.

But it was too late. Years too late. He'd promised Carrie. And he didn't make promises lightly. "It's just a whim, Bridge," he said, forcing himself to take another step back. "It'll pass."

"Just sex," she whispered again, her voice scarcely audible and so pleading that he could barely believe it had come from between her lips.

He tried to catch his breath and curb his runaway pulse, hardly wanting her to know his whole world was sliding sideways. "For one night? A week? While we're on this trip? Or until you get bored with me, the way you get bored with your boyfriends?"

Her jaw slackened and she looked stunned. "I can't believe you said that."

Did she really think she could involve him in a crazy love affair that would turn him to cinders and ash, like Forrest Hartley? His lips twisted in a wry smile. "I think you'd just wind up being sorry."

Her chin actually quivered, and while his heart went out to her, he wasn't going to let her jerk him around. She said, "If we don't try this, we'll never know if we'd be sorry."

"Let me get this straight," he said. "You're offering yourself to me for…"

Her voice sounded strained. "Tonight."

He tried not to think of the lonely nights he'd lain in bed after spending an evening with her, and yes…as much as he hated to admit it, he'd touched himself, *stroked* himself, until he'd come, over and over, always imagining he was suffering under the sweet torture of her hands. Inside, he was tied in knots. Anger and desire mixed together like cooking batter, until no ingredient was distinguishable from another. That they'd had such a strange night didn't help. He was still on hyper-alert from their run to the SUV. Maybe he was even still scared. "Tonight?"

"Tomorrow," she added, her voice still shaking. "If…"

He raised an eyebrow. "If?"

"We like it."

Oh, he was sure he'd like it. That wasn't the issue. "You're suggesting we amuse ourselves during our vacation down here, huh?" Eyeing her a long moment, he wrestled with the growing urge to torture her, just the way she'd tortured him for so long. Unable to stop himself, he came closer, intentionally pressing his erection against her, so she could feel what she was going to miss—the throbbing heat burgeoning through his pants. Watching with satisfaction as red color flushed her cheeks, he ducked his head, lowered his lips almost to hers and whispered, "Have you been having fantasies about me, Bridget?"

She inched back to better look at him, exposing a creamy neck he desperately wanted to sponge with his tongue, and his eyes settled on the pulse point, which was ticking wildly. "A few."

His voice lowered another notch, turning throatier. "And did you touch yourself, Bridge?" Had she aroused herself, just as he had?

She swallowed hard, her eyes widening. He barely heard her admit, "Yeah."

"Did you pretend it was me?"

Her eyes found his, and suddenly, he wasn't so proud of himself. The china-blue depths looked wounded, and as watery as the ghosts from which they'd just run. "Why are you doing this to me?"

"For the same reason you've done it to me for years." He could admit that much.

Her jaw hardened. "Well, the answer's yes," she muttered, her voice husky with fear and the night, with her arousal and anger. "Yes." Her eyes found his, and now they glinted with something darker than wounded injury. Only when she whispered, "You made me come in my fantasies," did he realize she was taking the upper hand, forcing him to imagine her, lying in bed in her apartment, unclothed, with her own hand gliding between her legs.

"Damn it," he suddenly whispered, his feelings about her tangled like a fine chain around his heart. What was wrong with him? Shouldn't he be thrilled? Hadn't he waited years for this?

His eyes drifted over her once more, roving over the skin of her cheeks, then the pink pursed dot of a mouth she'd just pressed to his. He could still feel the guilty pleasure of it. Carrie Masterson was waiting for him in New York, but… "You can't do this. Not now."

"Why not?"

Because it was just a whim for her. A stupid lark. Just a little fear on a February night mixed with a couple shots of good aged whiskey. "It's just the ghosts," he muttered.

She whispered back, "Yours or mine?"

Somehow, by some law of physics he'd never understand, his mind was pulling him away from her, but his mouth was only coming closer, his head angling farther down, their lips grazing. His head felt muzzy. "You're the one with the ghosts," he muttered gruffly, suddenly realizing his hand was still on her back. The heat of her skin was burning his palms, nothing more than the flutter of her breath seemed strong enough to knock him over. "All those men you've dated…"

"Just once," she whispered.

"And tomorrow?" he murmured. "If I want that, too?"

"Just while we're here."

Like a moment out of time. Maybe she'd intuited what was happening with him and Carrie. Maybe Bridge knew it was time for them to move on. And God knew, he wanted a few nights with her, with the slow burn of quiet desperation, if only because she'd always withheld herself and been so maddeningly unavailable.

She shifted, and the contact—thighs to thighs—was like a slow water torture she'd spent years perfecting just for him. The warmth of her belly seeped through his shirt, and the tips of her breasts were unbelievably hard, knotting against his chest.

"Okay," he muttered softly. And unable to take any more, he uttered a final grunt of useless protest, leaned, parted his lips, and entirely covered her mouth.

SHE MELTED, that hard, beautiful mouth giving her everything she wanted. She was still jittery from seeing the ghosts, and she still wasn't sure they were real—but she knew this was. Dermott was flesh and blood, and what she'd seen earlier was nothing compared to the light show exploding inside her now. The deepening kiss seemed to meld with the burning red light she'd witnessed in the liquid sky, and while her senses reeled, her own internal darkness edged outward, and she wondered why she'd been such a scared fool. Why hadn't she suggested this years ago?

But she'd never thought of Dermott like *that*— never allowed herself to do so—and so she hadn't expected the stark power of his body, the heat of his male flesh, nor the overwhelming thrust of his tongue. She felt crushed apart, strangely broken inside as the spear stroked her, exploring inside her mouth until nothing was untouched and she was gasping, screaming for him, teetering on the edge. Splaying fingers circled around her waist as if he'd touched her a thousand times already, his fingers digging hard into her skin, anxious to possess, forcing her hips to grind against an erection that was impossibly hot against her belly, the feel of it coming through her sweatpants like a brand.

Impulsively, she tightened her arms around his neck, and his lips slammed down harder, his tongue going wild with the kiss, his excitement like sparks in the middle of dry-heat lightning. A bolt of liquid desire claimed her core; something seemed to squirt inside her, and she gushed, her head flying back, so he could drip scalding kisses down her neck before another onslaught of his mouth. Every inch of her felt more energized, and yet felt weak. She had to lie down. The blood in her veins was quickening, her limbs turning languid.

With his mouth locked to hers, he pulled her toward the bed, and she raked at his waistband, pushing up his shirt, barely able to believe this. Was she really undressing Dermott? Was he really responding? Were they going to do it—or was one of them going to come to their senses and chicken out?

He urged her backward, and they went tumbling onto the mattress and then they were rolling. Belly brushed belly and she was stunned at the electricity, panting hard at the raw lightning zig-zagging into her extremities, making her gush with fire. She wanted...

He groaned. "Bridget."

It wasn't a statement, or a question, and she knew instinctively that he just needed to say her name. What he meant was "yes," and she took him at his word, stripping off his shirt, rubbing her palms over his pectorals, using her fingers to pinch his nipples...

She could hope Mug wouldn't come out to investigate the noise, not wanting anything to break this rhythm. And there *was* a rhythm. He was on top, their sweatpants no barrier. Suddenly, she remembered a pool party where he'd worn some of those decadently tight bikini-style trunks, which had shown off every blessed inch, and yes...right now she was experiencing the rush of feeling each inch that had tortured her imagination since that day.

"Oh, yes," she murmured, her hands wild in his hair. She'd fantasized about Dermott for days after the pool party, hadn't she? She'd imagined he'd come out of the pool, the tight wet black fabric clinging to him, and she'd knelt in front of him, her eyes feasting on the outline of his penis before her hands started exploring the long ridge, feeling it get harder against her massaging hand until Dermott was going crazy, widening his stance, the muscles of his legs hard as rocks, both his hands in her hair, grabbing it in fistfuls, while he begged and gasped...

But he was Dermott, her friend, which meant he was off-limits, and she couldn't really do anything. Not then. She was past all that now, and when she stripped off her own shirt, relief flooded her. She was going to have him tonight. Deep down, she'd wanted this for years. As he covered a breast, squeezing softly, he groaned against her mouth, offering another openmouthed kiss while using his fingers to explore a nipple. She arched, thrusting her seeking hips, her mind strangely muddled.

What was really happening here? She could almost believe the plantation house's magic was affecting them. Dermott was a flesh-and-blood man but the pleasure was too good to be real. No man's touch had ever done this to her. She'd got so hot, so wet. So afraid he'd stop. Men had done more. Kissed her more deeply, touched her more intimately, but she was climbing.

The grind of his hips brought his hard ridge against her, forcing open her folds, even through her clothes, finding her clitoris, and she cried out, the sound of her need surprising her. Rippling, twisting sensations filled her, sending her spiraling when his mouth left hers and locked onto a nipple. He was shuddering now, just as she was, sucking fast breaths between his teeth, his eyes as hot as fire during the one second he glanced up. They lasered into her flesh, burning like a light to show him the way as he followed it downward.

Whimpering, she simply couldn't believe the feel of his mouth. "It's like nothing before." And she knew it would be like nothing afterward, not this.

His tongue swirled, flicking the bud, and then he bit, his teeth capturing a sensitized tip. He tugged lightly, like a dog with a bone, then she felt a slow burn as he rubbed his chin between her breasts, nuzzling the cleavage with bearded stubble, roughening her skin, then inching lower, shaking his head back and forth as he did the same with her belly. A hot liquid tongue soothed everywhere his beard had burned, and she opened for him, parting her legs, stretching her knees as far as they'd go.

She whimpered as he yanked the drawstring of her sweatpants, his beard teasing her navel, the bristles so stiff and yet so soft, forcing her to arch senselessly, her overpowering physical neediness more than she could bear, her heart hammering as she felt his erection. It was lower now, fiery against her thigh, pressuring her through his pants, the thought of that hard flesh piercing her suddenly making her gasp.

Lifting her buttocks, she willed him to slide her pants down her legs, her heart swelling when she glanced down and saw his expression now—so sexy, so sincere—his hair mussed, his dark eyes glazed. When the pants were off, he stared down at the triangular silk scrap covering her, and he grunted softly with desire, his warm hand cupping her briefly, his palm grinding into her pelvis, his fingers curving until one settled at her opening and stroked damp silk, the finger bending more, vibrating. When he withdrew the touch, she felt so achy. So bereft. The string of the thong was drenched, her breath coming in fits she couldn't tame. She watched, unable to take her eyes off him, as he stripped down his own sweatpants, pushing them over his hips, exposing the thick tangle of black hair coating his thighs.

The shape of his erection was maddening. It strained against the fabric of his briefs, and it was so sexy to see him so aroused, knowing she was going to satisfy him. "Take them off," she gasped.

But his hand only covered the tiny triangle of blue panty again. "Turn over first," he whispered huskily. "Let me see you from the back." Heat flooding her, she did as he asked—she'd do absolutely anything he asked right now. Her neck craning to look at his face, she wasn't disappointed when she saw his eyes on fire with male approval.

A quivering palm ran over her bare backside, then he dipped a finger, found the back string of the thong, lifted it and gently pulled off the panties. As soon as they were gone, she twisted in his arms.

"You look amazing, Bridge," he said thickly, a soft pant following the words, and then a rasp sounded by her ear as he leaned downward, his tongue on her neck now, making a long blazing tongue trail as he got rid of his briefs. He fell to her then, his mouth wild on hers, and the hand that found her breast was just as excited, cupping and squeezing, lifting the flesh high, the heat of his unsheathed length burning her skin. Suddenly, it was too much. Enough foreplay. She was drenched and he was burning, and as if he'd read her mind, his eyes found hers.

"There's a condom in my bag," she managed.

He was gone in a flash. She drank in his nude body, feeling stunned admiration as she took in the broad shoulders, tapering torso and long legs. How could he be Dermott? She could barely believe this was happening as he found her bag, rifled through it, and returned. Her heart seemed to stop. For a second, she really couldn't breathe. He was so perfect. Ready. Straight as an arrow. The whole front of his body was coated with hair. He came toward her opening the packet, and she watched as he put on the condom, rolling it down the length. Her body was feverish, burning all over, her breasts aroused, hungry for his mouth again. She held out her arms, inviting him.

He accepted, lying down and wasting no time. Uttering a soft sob, she felt him enter her, the long thrust spreading her inside, taking away her breath. When he was all the way in, she felt his hand curl under her chin, and when he spoke, his voice was a rough rasp. "Bridge?"

It was so intense. Just staring into his eyes like this, with him so deep inside her. "Yeah."

"Are you ready?"

She knew just what he meant. Her fingers curled around his shoulders, the smoothness shocking her, as if she'd expected his skin to be as rough as his chest or beard, and she kept her eyes on his as he slowly withdrew. When his body fully left hers, a cry was torn from her throat, and she jerked her head away, but the hand found her chin again, pulling her gaze back to his. Just as slowly, he pushed inside, the thickness of him stretching her, parting her until she was sure she'd burst, each blessed ridge burning. He felt like steel. He entered her so incredibly slowly that she was almost crying.

"Tease me," she whispered, because he already was, using just the heated tip at the opening. Keeping her stretched and ready, he ground against her, so she'd feel the shaft against her clitoris, and when she parted farther, silently begging for more, he gave it.

Those eyes, she thought. Dermott's eyes. They were dark, beautiful eyes she'd peered into for over twenty years, and yet she felt she'd never seen them. He'd only been her friend before; now they were lovers.

"How's that feel, Bridge? Okay?"

Perfect. Amazing. Beyond anything I'd imagined. "Good," she managed, her eyes suddenly shutting, the sensations too overpowering. More so, as he speeded their rhythm, his thrusts turning hard and fast, his nipples brushing hers, the contact sending her into nowhere. The evening no longer existed— not the drive, or Zechariah Walsh or the ghosts and fireworks. All that mattered was heat and flesh. She had to arch, higher and faster, to capture each thrust. And when his mouth found hers again, the kiss swirled inside her mind, melting like ice cream on a hot day. She seized. Her body convulsed, shuddering in his strong arms, even as he kept bearing her upward, still pummeling her while she shook with release, so it felt as if she'd never stop coming, and then he let go, uttering just one harsh male sound.

Vaguely, she realized they were locked around each other tightly, their legs and arms cradling. Despite the room's chill, their bodies were hot, damp with exertion and filling the room with the pungent scent of love. "I don't know what to say," she managed, her breath only a pant.

"Nothing, Bridge," he murmured. And then he merely pulled her even closer and started kissing her again.

5

CALM DOWN, Bridget coached herself early the next morning as she held a jacket over her head, shielding herself from the rain as she speeded her steps, jogging across the motel parking lot. Leaping over puddles and trying to ignore the darker clouds that were rolling in, she kept her eyes fixed on Nancy's Diner. *You're acting like a crazy woman,* she thought. *Like exactly the kind of woman your mother always taught you to loathe.*

But how could she help it? Dermott was amazing, as it turned out. Bridget had never had sex like that. It had taken everything she had not to call her sisters and report the news, but Dermott was right. Kissing and telling was rude. Still…he'd gone all night, and now her insides felt positively mushy, not to mention her heart. As she blinked, batting away raindrops with her eyelashes, she scanned the gray sky, the two-block long main drag of Big Swamp, which was dotted with mom-and-pop businesses, then the cars in the lot. Dermott's SUV was still here! He hadn't left her, after all!

"Of course he hasn't," she muttered. He'd never abandon her. The closest thing to it was his distanced treatment of her lately. Tasting raindrops as they caught on her lips, she wondered what was wrong with her. She'd never acted with this level of insecurity, and certainly not when a man was involved.

She forced herself to stop. And then she started walking. Slowly. In a dignified manner. Despite the rain. No man, not even Dermott, was going to turn her into a lunatic. Her sister, Edie, was the hopeless romantic, the kind of woman who'd lose her head over a man. No…Edie was light-years from knowing how to control men with their mother's or Marley's dexterity. Viv had countless ways of making their dad do things for her, and most of the time Joe Benning didn't even realize he was being seriously manipulated. Marley was astute with men, too, not that she'd ever found anyone permanent, of course, but that was only because of the curse, something Bridget intended to rectify, maybe this morning. Surely, the ring was in Granny Ginny's house, but how was Bridget supposed to find it?

She could only hope for divine intervention. She was under time pressure, too. If Carrie Masterson called one more time, she was going to scream. She just wished her mind wasn't running wild. When she'd awakened with only Mug for company, her first thought was that Dermott had gone back to New York, paying her back for her previous unwillingness to explore the physical side of their relationship. Was he trying to point out her obvious stupidity? After all, if she'd had any idea how good sex would be, she'd have pursued it long before now, friendship be damned.

"He's here," she whispered again. "So calm down." How long had he been gone? She had no way of knowing, since she'd slept like the dead. Between the shock of seeing what might have been ghosts, followed by Dermott's lovemaking, her overtaxed body and subconscious had needed extra process time. Where was he?

Oh. There. She could see him through the fogged window of the diner, in deep conversation with Nancy. Blowing out a relieved sigh as Nancy moved away, carrying a half-full coffeepot and Dermott's finished plate, Bridget was aware that her heart was hammering. Swallowing to soothe the dryness of her constricted throat, she pushed through the door of the diner, only to have every customer on the orange swivel stools turn to stare. That's when she realized she'd worn another outfit that wasn't quite right for Big Swamp, Florida: black tights, witch boots and a lace blouse that showed too much skin. Her fake tattoo, an ivy vine circling her neck, probably didn't help matters.

"I guess you believe the stories about the hauntings now," someone chortled.

And then everyone laughed. Taking a deep breath, she realized no response was necessary, and as the customers turned around once more, she beelined for Dermott's booth. His laptop was open on the table. Since he'd finished breakfast, she did her best not to look upset. "You already ate?"

His tone was chilly. "Is there something wrong with that?"

So, he was spoiling for a fight. She scooted farther

into her side of the booth, and after shaking rain from her jacket, she placed it beside her. She was just about to answer when Nancy did another table-sweep. "Coffee, hon?"

"Please."

Bridget waited dutifully while Nancy sloshed suspiciously watery-looking coffee into a cup, mentally noting that the morning's wake-up jolt was going to lack the bang of her usual double-shot lattes. When Nancy slid a waxy oversize menu across the orange Formica tabletop, Bridget said, "Thanks," and when she was gone, continued, "You could have gotten me up, you know." Hadn't Dermott wanted to be with her this morning?

He was eyeing her, not looking particularly pleased, which wasn't a good sign, but she didn't know what she'd done wrong. "You're up now."

Great. Dermott usually wasn't the withholding type, but this morning, he wasn't going to divulge whatever was on his mind. She simply couldn't believe this. Wishing she could better control her frustrated sighs and the exaggerated movements of her hands, since they exposed her annoyance and made her look foolish, she opened the menu and stared at it, unseeing, suddenly not caring what she ate. If Dermott really cared about her, he'd have awakened her and spent the morning in bed.

She shut the menu. "I hope I'm not intruding."

Even though he knew exactly what she meant, he said, "Don't be ridiculous, Bridge."

Ah. So, his surly attitude was in her imagination? She felt her temper rise a notch. She couldn't help but cross her arms over her waist. There was nothing she hated more than passive-aggressive, especially since she couldn't point to exactly what Dermott had done wrong. She had stellar gut instincts, though. Hers were saying he'd purposely avoided her, and her feelings were hurt, but he wanted to deny it completely. Was he sorry they'd made love? Just as she parted her lips to ask, Nancy returned, and Bridget wound up ordering instead while Dermott turned his attention to the open laptop.

"No more grits and gravy?" Nancy teased.

"They were wonderful," Bridget assured, mustering a convincing expression as she handed the menu to Nancy, "but just toast this morning, please." As Nancy headed toward the kitchen, Bridget glanced at Dermott. Warring emotions tumbled inside her. The first was anger, because he was staring intently at the computer screen. At any other time in their relationship, she wouldn't have cared. In fact, like most women, she'd sat through countless male obsessions: Nintendo, Monday Night Football and prize fights. Watching men surf the net was nothing new. Still, Dermott was ruining this. All night long they'd been sweating, panting and writhing on a vibrating bed, and while she hated to morph into such a girl-type girl, especially since they'd been buddies for so many years, she did think the experience rated at least one dazzling smile, or a simple sentence of commentary, which would go something like, "Did I ever tell you that you're wonderful, Bridget?"

Vaguely, she wondered if she could send her father, Joe, after Dermott with a shotgun. A smile tugged her lips. Or better yet, her biological father. Smiling, thinking of how steady Joe was, she could hardly believe her mother had once married a hellion. But judging from the bumper stickers on cars in the lot, the South produced a lot of them. Around here, a man wouldn't be a man unless he had some machismo on his résumé.

Her pique with Dermott didn't last. Simultaneously, she melted. Dermott looked so well-loved and gorgeous this morning, after all. He was wearing worn black jeans with gaping holes in the knees; a navy nylon zippered jacket that was open over a tight white T-shirt which outlined every inch of his chest. Between his pecs hung a thick gold chain of the sort favored by hip-hop stars; she'd given it to him to mark the anniversary of their first meeting. At the thought, her heart suddenly flip-flopped. Before last night, he'd only kissed her once, when they'd first met. He'd been five years old.

The day after the Brandts had moved next door, Mrs. Benning had invited Mrs. Brandt to bring her son to the Bank Street playground, which left its sprinklers running in the summer for the kids. Bridget had been wearing bikini bottoms, and Dermott had been wearing his underwear, since his mother hadn't finished unpacking and couldn't find his swim trunks.

Or so the story went. Much of the day was hazy in Bridget's memory, but she did remember the end. It was early evening, and she and her new playmate were about to be separated forever. Her stomach was rumbling because it was past dinnertime, and yet she didn't want to leave because it was such a perfect day, with clouds tinged with twilight and a breeze blowing down Bank Street from the Hudson. Not realizing they lived next door, Dermott kissed her goodbye as if they were never to meet again.

She'd fallen in love at that moment. He'd created a soft space inside her that no one else would ever be able to touch, and they'd been friends ever since. Now the eyes he'd kept trained on the laptop looked heavy-lidded. His still-mussed hair carried the comb-marks of her fingers, and the Fu Manchu goatee would be a full beard if he didn't shave before tonight. "Couldn't you sleep?" she suddenly asked. Was that why he was so surly?

He glanced up, his lips pursing slightly. "I slept just fine."

"Doubtful," she countered. "You're being *trés* moody."

"I'm downloading a recording."

Was that any reason to ignore her? Before she thought it through, she leaned forward. "Look," she muttered, keeping her voice low, so any gossips in the diner couldn't hear. "I've watched you over the years. We're not exactly strangers, you know. And every time you're around a woman you don't want to deal with, you bury yourself in work. So, I know what you're up to. Don't do it to me, Dermott."

His jaw set. He leaned forward, too. "What?" he countered, peering at her over the top edge of the laptop. "Do you think I'm not dealing with what happened last night?"

"Now we're getting somewhere," she said, nodding.

"You couldn't be more wrong, Bridget."

He was such a liar. Even with the table between them, he was close enough that she could smell his body, and the scent of it flooded her mind with memories—his knee between her legs, his fingers probing her, the warm spear of his tongue in her ear before he whispered, "You're making me feel so good tonight."

She swallowed hard. In her mind's eye, she was seeing his naked, aroused flesh, and recalling how it had felt to have the power of arousing him, knowing she was satisfying his most basic needs. She blew out a shaky breath, since it was the wrong time to feel rushing spirals of heat whirling into her blood, not that she could help the response now, nor the way her breasts peaked against her top, feeling achy and raw. Her breath caught. "Am I wrong?" she managed to counter.

As if he wouldn't even grace her taunting question with a response, he glanced at the laptop again, then suddenly spun it, so that she could see the screen, pressing a button to activate the media player. In the next instant, she almost forgot their argument. "What..." she whispered.

He pressed a finger to his lips. "Sh...listen."

Tilting her head closer, since the speaker was turned down low, she attended to the sounds. Hooves thundered, rifles fired. Whirring shells zipped through the air. A ka-boom sounded. Then another. She frowned as Dermott rewound and played a segment again. It sounded so familiar.

She gasped, her eyes locking onto his. "That's what we heard last night." As they'd run from her grandmother's house, she'd heard these same sounds, in exactly this sequence. There was gunfire first, then galloping horses, followed by gunshots and cannonballs. She squinted, silently asking for an explanation.

"It's part of the sound track to *Gone with the Wind.*"

She couldn't believe it. "The movie?"

He nodded. "It was bugging me all night."

She tried not to take offense. "All night?"

He ignored the reference. "I kept thinking I'd heard those sounds before."

"You know more about movies than anyone I've ever met." If anybody could have figured this out, it was Dermott.

"Someone found a way to play the sound track at your grandmother's. Which proves what we heard last night isn't the product of the supernatural, Bridget."

Relief flooded her, but only for a moment. On its heels, came a swift drop in mood, as if someone had pulled the proverbial rug out from under her. The disappointment was intense. "If that's true, it also discounts everything else Granny Ginny said." Bridget didn't want to believe this was all a hoax, not really. It simply couldn't be. Looking into Dermott's gaze, she'd never been more sure of the existence of the wedding curse. Yeah, the proof was right in front of her.

How could a man have such mind-blowing sex with her and not seem more affected than this?

Oblivious of her thoughts, he said, "So, the way I see it, our next move is to talk to the people who might bear a grudge against your grandmother, or have something to gain financially if she sells her property. Nancy says the pawnbroker, Garth Cousins, has a shop a few doors down on Main Street, and while she wouldn't say more, I think there are rumors about the relationship between the Cousins family and the Hartleys. Mavis Benchley volunteers at the library every morning. It's across town, Nancy said, but around here, that means less than a mile. We might as well walk."

He looked ready to go. Bridget could barely believe he didn't simply close his laptop, shove it under his arm and bolt for the door. Somehow, she forced herself to take a deep breath. So much for sex this morning. Or even a warm, loving smile. Or even decent conversation. Her voice was tinged with annoyance. "I hate to be difficult, but do you mind if I *eat*?"

In the pregnant pause that ensued, whole worlds seemed to pass between them, and she couldn't help but wonder if they were going to talk about this cataclysmic shift in their relationship at all.

"Of course you can eat," he finally said.

Nancy could not have timed her arrival any better. It was the perfect moment for her to put down Bridget's toast plate with a clank. After that, there was a moment's reprieve from the tension, as if Nancy had cut through everything whirling between her and Dermott—all the sexual vibrations, electricity, uncertainty and confusion.

But that was only the calm before the storm, because at the very next moment, Dermott's phone jangled, and it was Carrie.

"WELL, I'll be a spotted hyena," Garth Cousins muttered in astonishment a half hour later, just moments after they'd pushed past the smudged glass door to his shop and come inside, leaving a long string of brass bells hanging from the doorknob to clank in their wake. Bridget had gone back to the motel briefly, just long enough to get Mug, while Dermott, not trusting himself to be in a room with both Bridget and a bed, waited for her outside. He'd also let her eat alone, calling Carrie from the SUV. Now he watched as she crooked a thumb toward the grungy plate-glass windows and a sign that said, No Dogs Allowed.

Lifting Mug, she promised, "He's not really a dog."

The man, who could have doubled for Grizzly Adams, surveyed Mug a long moment, then said gruffly, "I imagine you're right, young lady. That pug dog looks more like a swamp rat to me."

It was the first thing that had broken Bridget's mood since she'd stormed into the diner. She laughed, delighted. Ducking her head, she whispered, "Did you hear that, Muggy Puggy? You're a swamp rat!" Excited by the idea, Mug yipped happily at the attention and wagged his tail wildly.

Dermott glanced around the shop, taking in the crammed cases of knives, guns, coins and estate jewelry, and when his gaze returned to Bridget, he realized the proprietor had crossed the shop, grasped her hand and brought it close to his lips, as if to kiss it. A protest died on Dermott's own, taking a back seat to curiosity, since Bridget was being treated like visiting royalty. It wasn't the hand that intrigued the man, though, it was the bauble on Bridget's finger.

The man whistled. "My, oh, my. That sure is purdy."

"Thanks."

"Garth Cousins," he said. "You can call me Garth. I'd heard a Hartley girl was in town," he continued, speaking around the unlit corncob pipe in his mouth. "But nobody mentioned that this gem had been found."

"You seem to have quite the rumor mill around here," Bridget commented.

He merely laughed, still squinting down at the ring. "You're here, I take it, to sell this so that you can pay taxes on the old homestead."

Bridget glanced toward Dermott, and he almost wished she hadn't. As they'd walked from the diner to the shop, he'd kept waiting for her to force the issue and demand to hear how he felt about their night together. The fact was, he had no idea. Oh, he wanted her. This morning, he'd stood beside the bed, his eyes drinking in every naked inch. He'd gaze-cruised her slender feet, the blue-painted toes, the sloping curves of her calves and thighs. When he'd reached the trimmed V of pubic hair, he'd felt a rush of remembered pleasure, and he'd started to get hard again. Seriously hard. He'd been thinking about making love to her ever since. Her breasts hadn't helped. They'd been uncovered this morning, her skin milky white. Relaxed, the nipples were soft and pink, tempting him to use his mouth to turn them red and pebbly again.

He'd fed Mug instead, and then he'd gotten the hell out of the motel. Now he told himself what happened with Bridget was just a one-time thing. Well, maybe a two-time thing. Just a fling for the few days they were here, just as she'd said. After all, if she'd wanted more from him, she would have asked a long time ago. Yeah, it was better just to play things by ear. Maybe, just maybe, he'd take a little more of what he now so desperately wanted from Bridget...

Bridget's voice brought him back to the present. "Thank you for admiring the ring," she said, "but it's made of..."

"Cubic zirconias," Garth Cousins announced happily, releasing her hand and pulling thoughtfully on a scraggly gray beard as he steered Bridget toward an old rocking chair in a corner of the shop and sat opposite her, on a dusty, gold-upholstered love seat.

Dermott followed, leaning against a showcase.

Arranging Mug in her lap, Bridget asked, "How did you know they weren't real diamonds?"

The elderly man's eyes slid to the cases of estate jewelry and then, looking offended, he returned his gaze to Bridget. "This is my business, Bridget."

"Of course," she said quickly. Then she sucked in a quick breath. "You know my name?"

It was his turn to look surprised. "'Course I do. Seen so many pictures of you that you could be my own daughter. Your first day of school, you wore your hair in a cute little pixie cut, and you wore a bright white dress you picked out yourself at Macy's, covered with a daisy print. And it seems to me…" He glanced at Dermott. "That this fellow escorted you right to the door of first grade. In the picture, I think Mr. Brandt was wearing a pair of spanking new jeans and a little striped seersucker coat, at least if memory serves me correctly." Taking the corncob pipe from between his lips, he grinned broadly. "But at my age, I wouldn't vouch for my memory."

Bridget's voice quickened. "How do you know all that?"

The old man was frowning. "Didn't Ginny tell you?"

She leaned forward, as if thinking exactly what Dermott was—that Granny Ginny hadn't told them half the information they needed. "Tell me what?"

Garth considered a moment, long enough that Dermott could get a better look at him. He was quite a character, dressed in worn-over alligator boots and blue jeans held up by a wide hand-tooled belt with a heavy hunk of turquoise on the buckle. Navajo beads hung around his neck, over a neatly pressed plaid shirt. Finally, he said the last thing Dermott expected. "Uh…I'm Ginny's boyfriend."

Bridget blinked rapidly, digesting the information and trying not to look rude. "Her boyfriend?" she echoed. "Uh…I hate to say it, but Granny Ginny never mentioned you to me."

"She likes to keep her love life private," explained Garth, "so I'm not that surprised. I guess it started after her husband died. By her husband, I mean Jasper's father. You see, Ginny and I started dating only three months after he'd passed, and we wanted to keep it under wraps, so the townsfolk wouldn't talk. You wouldn't believe how folks in Big Swamp gossip."

"Oh," assured Bridget, "I think we might. Everybody in town knows Dermott and I are here. Zechariah Walsh heard from people in the diner, and when we showed up at the motel, they already had a room waiting."

Dermott suddenly realized he'd been staring at her again, and he shifted his attention to the shop, which was full of curiosities, everything from antiques to carved scrimshaw and handwoven Native American baskets and rugs. In her tights and flowing lace top, Bridget looked as if she'd just stepped from another time period. His chest constricted, and he found himself thinking of the Christmas party at Tiffany's again. She'd been dressed for romance on that evening, also.

Her listener looked every bit as captivated as himself as she plunged into the story of their adventures at the plantation house, including Dermott's recent discovery that the sounds they'd thought were ghosts were really the *Gone with the Wind* sound track. "That doesn't explain the visual apparitions, of course," she finished. "Dermott's convinced there's a reasonable explanation, though…"

As her voice trailed off, Garth leaned back, clapping a hand decisively on a wide, hand-carved cherrywood arm. "I don't mean to burst your bubble," he began, repositioning the pipe and glancing between Bridget and Dermott. "But you kids better be careful. Lavinia Delroy always swore that the devil's handiwork was in that place. Forrest and Miss Marissa died there, sure enough, and don't you kid yourselves. They still walk the floors at night. So does Ginny's son. I've no idea why the sounds you heard match those on a movie sound track, but whatever the case, I assure you that old place is overrun with ghosts.

"I stayed out there one night with your granny," he continued, focusing his attention on Bridget, "and once was enough for me. I vowed never to do it again. I said, 'Ginny, honey, if you want company, you're going to have to visit the apartment above the shop in Big Swamp.' You'd better believe it, kids, I've been trying to get her off that property for years."

"That's what we heard," Dermott cut in, if only because speaking got his mind off Bridget. "But we thought you wanted the timber. That's what Ginny said."

"That's true," agreed Garth.

Before he could further explain, Bridget interjected, saying, "This is so strange. Dermott and I had no idea you were nearly a relation."

"Not only am I close to Ginny, but our families go back a-ways, too. The Cousins have been in these parts as long as the Hartleys, and we were pawnbrokers in Big Swamp long before it became a reputable occupation. This building dates back before the war. 'Course, it's changed quite a bit, but the space above the shop used to be a house of ill repute. My great-great-great grandfather was the first to start buying up Hartley jewelry, mostly pieces Lavinia had hid upstairs under the floorboards in what's now your granny's room. She did it the night Yankees came, before she and Marissa fled to the swamp.

"But then you probably know all that. No doubt Ginny's told you about the chandelier, too. I'm not the only man she's begged to try to take it down. But it just won't budge. It's rooted in the ceiling and never intends to leave."

"You couldn't get it down?" Bridget asked breathlessly.

He shook his head. "No way. Neither could the Yankees. Anyway, after the war, the relatives came back, found the hidden jewelry and sold it piece by piece. Nobody could afford to hire labor to work all those fields. Back in those days, Hartleys owned more than Ginny's got now. They had part of Benchley property, as well as a spread across the swamps that went to a land developer at the turn of the century. That's the root of the Benchley-Hartley feud, you know. Mavis and Ginny have a long-standing dispute over the property line.

"At any rate, if Ginny didn't mention it, Cousins men have been buying Hartley jewelry for years. The proceeds are what's been paying her property taxes. Your granny's never worked a day in her life, Bridget, and as far as I'm concerned, a pretty woman such as her wasn't made for toil."

His voice drifted off as he thought of Ginny. "Thing is," he continued abruptly, as if realizing he'd lost the thread of conversation, "Ginny's husband was no good, nor was her son." He paused. "No offense to your daddy's memory, Bridget, but the man who raised you was a better deal. Your mother's first husband was charming as the devil himself, so it's no wonder he captured her heart, but he was bad with money, gambled on horses and he loved to drink. It was only a matter of time until he started keeping women on the side, too, I'll wager. Be that as it may, women always fell for him like a ton of bricks.

"Anyway, after her husband was gone, your granny was strapped for cash. And that's where I came in. She came into Big Swamp—under the cover of night, mind you—to pawn the last of the jewelry Lavinia had hidden during the war, and that's when she met me. As far as our romance goes, the spark was kindled and the rest is history. Meantime…" He rose and said, "Well, follow me."

Curious, Dermott followed Garth and Bridget to a back room where Garth spun the combination to a massive walk-in safe, opened the door and urged them inside. "The Hartley jewelry," he said simply.

Rows of dazzling rings and brooches lined the velvet shelf to which he pointed. Dermott's eyes widened, and when he glanced at Bridget, his heart squeezed tight. He'd never seen her look so completely enchanted. Or maybe he had. Last night, when he'd thrust deeply inside her, his hand cupping her chin, urging her to look into his eyes while they made love, her eyes had possessed this same astonished look of wonder.

"You have it all?" she whispered. "How's that possible? Didn't anyone ever come in and buy the pieces after you and your relatives had bought them from Granny's estate?"

"Oh, sure," Garth said. "But…" His eyes lit up as brightly as the dazzling diamonds he'd collected.

"Well…you can't tell your granny, not yet, but I've slowly bought back most of the pieces over the years. I figured—" His voice suddenly cracked. "If she ever says she'll have me, well…"

Bridget's lips parted. "They're going to be a gift?" He nodded.

"How sweet," Bridget gushed.

"The only piece of Hartley jewelry that's still missing is the original of the ring you're wearing," he explained. "Like I said, your granny's convinced that the Hartley House ghosts are appearing in your dreams, even if you can't remember them. It's happened to your granny, you know."

"She said that's why I was able to design a replica of a ring I'd never seen," Bridget murmured.

"If the ring's ever found," Garth clarified, "selling it would bring enough money to pay the outstanding bills on the plantation—"

"She owes money?" Bridget interjected.

"Tons," Garth assured. "But even if the ring was found, Ginny would never sell. She's convinced that keeping the ring in the family is necessary to end the curse. It needs to stay where it belongs, in the home Miss Marissa was to have shared with Forrest."

Bridget blew out a frustrated sigh. "Where is it?"

"I don't know. But selling it would keep her property from government seizure for a while, but she'd never sell it because she wants to ensure your future happiness. And that's why I want her to harvest all that hardwood. I wish you'd talk her into selling it. She says she loves her trees too much, but they're worth a lot."

"Wow," Bridget said simply, looking impressed.

Dermott felt the same. And then he startled. He'd scarcely been aware of it, but he'd actually been imagining finding the diamond and putting it on Bridget's finger. Had he gone crazy?

"I don't believe in ghosts," he assured the pair, coming to his senses and leveling Garth with a practical stare. "I really did download the sounds we heard, and they're definitely from a movie sound track. That means there's got to be an explanation for the apparitions we saw."

Garth sighed as if to say elderly folks had no choice other than to let the young make their own mistakes, then he said, "Have it your way, son." He paused delicately. "Tell you what," he continued amiably, as if he wasn't about to argue. "I'd love to see more of you. And Ginny would kill me if all you got to eat while you were here was Nancy's greasy ham and eggs. So, why don't you plan on coming back later for victuals? I cook up a soul-food dinner that's not to be believed. While I do the shopping, you can continue with your…uh…research expedition. If you're really convinced this is a hoax, and that somebody's out to get Ginny, you'd better talk to Mavis Benchley."

Dermott watched as the man's face hardened. "She's the only person I know who's mean and vindictive enough actually to try to run your granny out of her hometown."

6

THE TINY, two-room library in Big Swamp had tall windows, old wooden desks, green banker's lamps, and a large sign in front that said Benchley Library, since, as it turned out, the structure had been built from funds donated by Benchleys. Moments before, right after she'd tied Mug's leash to a parking meter and entered the library with Dermott, Bridget had told herself she was almost glad he'd had the nerve to abandon her in the diner, call Carrie instead of sharing breakfast and wait outside the motel room while she got Mug. Did he really fear Bridget might force a conversation about their relationship once inside the privacy of a bedroom? Was her previous best friend, now lover, really that spineless?

So be it.

Yes…she'd be glad to act as if the night she and Dermott had spent together was as inconsequential as he wanted to make it seem. She'd give him a taste of his own medicine. Oh-so-casually turning her body from him now, she lavished all her attention on Mavis Benchley, who was staring at the ring. "You're sure you've never seen a picture of this?" Mavis demanded.

"Positive."

"Really? Because I know Miss Marissa's wearing it in the portrait in Ginny's parlor."

For an archenemy, Mavis sure knew her way around Bridget's grandmother's home, something that sent up warning flags. "You've visited Granny's house? I didn't think you two got along."

"I've heard descriptions," Mavis explained.

Bridget could buy that, given what she'd seen of the Big Swamp gossip mills. Ginny probably knew Mavis's household, as well, right down to the count of the silver spoons. "I see."

Mavis shook her head in wonderment. "Hmm. You never saw the ring, but dreamed of the design? I'm sure I'm not the first to tell you, but that means you've probably had a visitation from Lavinia."

"Not so far," interjected Bridget. "But I had a dream in which I thought I was Miss Marissa."

"Don't fool yourself. That could easily be Lavinia's doing. It's hard to tell, since she's a wily one. To answer some of your questions about the Hartley household," continued Mavis, pointing toward a display case, "I'm afraid this is all we have left of Lavinia Delroy." Her tone was apologetic, but her eyes had narrowed to wary slits; she clearly wasn't about to forget that she was dealing with a woman cursed with Hartley blood. "At least all we have of Lavinia," she amended, "that can be viewed by the tax-paying public."

Bridget was sure some jab at Ginny was meant. Ignoring it, she studied some fabric dolls that were almost as small as South American worry dolls. Made of black burlap, they were stuffed with straw and had buttons for eyes. "Interesting."

"Lavinia made them by hand. And this—" Mavis pointed. "Is one of the original pouches in which she carried her herbs. We have modern examples of the herbs, too, and you'll recognize their names, since they're sold in health food stores today. St. John's Wort, Kava Kava…"

Mavis hesitated. "If you look in your granny's attic, you'll find the real treasures. I've asked her to contribute family papers to the library, but she says she won't trust Benchleys with them. To tell you the truth, I'd never trust your grandmother, either, and I have better reasons than she.

"Still, about a month ago, I said to her, 'Ginny, why can't we just bury the hatchet? We're older now. Neither of us is married, not really. Neither of us has kids, although she's got you and your sisters up north. Still, someone in Big Swamp needs to ensure that our legacies live on.' Well, Ginny told me that she has Miss Marissa and Lavinia's diaries, as well as books of old photographs. She said they're in a big steamer trunk in the attic, and there are enough old gowns that we could display them in glass cases and really dress this place up, so to speak. You know, gowns that old go for a fortune, museums even want them for display, but…" Her voice hardened. "Ginny just won't give anything to a Benchley."

Bridget tried not to take offense. After all, the Ginny Hartley she knew was kind, if a little batty. Besides, to look at Mavis, it was hard to imagine why Ginny hadn't taken to Mavis like a bee to honey, since no two women could have looked more alike. Both were elderly and still enjoying good health. Both were petite, with blond ringlets and lily skin. Both favored pastel suits with two-tone pumps. They could have been sisters. "I know my grandmother," Bridget ventured, vaguely aware that Dermott was behind her, still examining the display cases. Shifting her weight to show a little more leg, she hoped he was eating his heart out. "And she loves history. I can't imagine she'd refuse to display family documents."

"Well," returned Mavis with a sniff, "that's only because you don't know about all the Hartley-Benchley troubles."

"Not so," Bridget countered, her eyes drifting down Mavis's powder-blue suit, then returning to a brooch on the collar that looked heavier than Mavis herself. She wasn't even five feet tall, which was why Bridget found herself stooping to peer into the woman's green eyes. "Granny's told me a lot."

"Oh, really?"

Bridget was beginning to think Garth had a point regarding Mavis Benchley's personality; her tone was insinuating, as if she knew plenty of things that Bridget didn't. "Yes, really," Bridget said.

"Then did Ginny happen to mention that Garth Cousins used to be my husband?"

Behind her, she heard Dermott's soft chuckle, and Bridget had to fight the impulse to turn around and kick him. This was certainly a new twist. Bridget frowned, hardly wanting to think about the implications of two women wanting the same man. "Your *husband?*"

"Separated, not divorced, so it's up to you to decide. Now, I wouldn't go so far as to say your granny stole him out from under me," Mavis clarified in a soft drawl that had a thread of steel running through it. "But Garth and I were only recently separated when she began seeing him."

"Which was?"

"About forty years ago. It wasn't long after her own husband died, and before your mother married her son, so Ginny was stuck with high overhead and a tax bill. Her ne'er-do-well son was hardly going to help. That's when she went to Garth to pawn some of the jewelry left from the war, and then, well..."

"Ah," Bridget couldn't help but murmur, barely aware she was speaking out loud, "so, the dispute's not a matter of ancient history, but a bit more recent?" If one could call forty years ago recent. Mavis and Garth must have married and separated at some point. Probably in a town this small, the breakup would have put Mavis in a bad light. To this day, Ginny was trying to keep her own affair private. Setting her jaw, Bridget told herself she'd have to have a little chat with Ginny. She hardly appreciated being sent to Big Swamp with partial information.

Mavis was eyeing her. "You were saying?"

"Well, I'd heard the problem between the two families stemmed from a property-line dispute."

"That, too."

"And then there was the issue of your family's refusal to hide Lavinia and Marissa, which is why they died in the swamp, right?"

Mavis gasped. "Now, there's a Hartley myth! I can't say we solicited our neighbors, to be sure. But if Lavinia and Marissa had shown up, the Benchleys would have taken them in. We were feuding about the property line before the war, and the Benchleys figured those women were too proud to seek charity."

Bridget could see this would quickly get into a circular argument, leading nowhere. "Garth and Ginny say you're the only one who might hold a grudge against Ginny, and I guess you've explained why. Now, here's the thing. Dermott and I were worried that you might be pretending to haunt my grandmother's property, out of spite."

Mavis reached a hand out instinctively, to brace herself against one of the cases. "Me? *Pretend* to haunt Ginny's place?" Her eyes implored Bridget's. "Why, you're as crazy as the rest of the Hartleys. Ginny's property is overrun with ghosts. That's not my doing. I can hear the hoopla from a mile away, so if you ask me, there oughtta be special zoning laws for haunted houses. And by the way," she added, "Zechariah Walsh is on my side in the matter."

"But the sounds aren't ghosts," Bridget argued. "Dermott recognized them. They're from the *Gone with the Wind* sound track."

Mavis's lips parted in surprise. "What, Missy?"

Dermott broke in, explaining, then he said, "So, if the sounds are manufactured, that means the apparitions must be, too."

Mavis looked about as convinced as her estranged husband. "I've no doubt that you believe that, but my family's been around since before the war. And…well, I don't know how to put this." She paused delicately. "Benchleys and Hartleys were hearing those sounds long before the Internet or Margaret Mitchell."

Glancing between Bridget and Dermott, Mavis said in what seemed a complete nonsequitur, "Are you two getting married?"

Bridget almost choked, and she wasn't about to turn around to gauge Dermott's reaction. "Uh…no. Of course not."

Once more, Mavis didn't look convinced. "Rumor has it that you two have known each other since kindergarten, and that you shared a room at the motel last night. Maybe you're just living together in sin or something, but my point is this, you don't have a chance together until you find the original Hartley ring. Until then, all Hartley romances are cursed, and everybody knows it."

Bridget was getting tired of her imperious tone. "I hate to mention it," she countered, "but Granny has a…" She searched for the right word. "Beau."

"One she can never marry," Mavis responded primly.

Bridget squinted. "Why?"

The thin line of Mavis's pink mouth stretched into an even thinner line that was meant to be a smile. "Because until she donates the papers in her attic to the Benchley Library, I won't divorce Garth."

A long silence fell. Then Bridget blew out a long breath and said, "If nothing else, the feud is starting to make a lot better sense."

Mavis wasn't deterred. "When you go back to Ginny's, get those papers out of the steamer trunk. Maybe you'll find a clue as to the whereabouts of the ring." Once more, she glanced between Bridget and Dermott, and then, as if willing herself to be kinder, she added, "Good luck with finding that ring. If you want any kind of future together, you'll need it."

Slowly, keeping her features masked, Bridget managed to turn and face Dermott, hoping to assure him that marriage was the last thing on her mind. After all, he didn't even seem to want to sleep with her again.

"GRANNY GINNY'S not back yet, Mom?" Bridget moaned many hours later, feeling impatient and still trying to suppress memories of Mavis Benchley's commentary, something Bridget and Dermott had avoided talking about after leaving the library. Fighting a shiver in the coolness of the room, she glanced toward the fireplace. Earlier, while she was showering, Dermott had built a fire, but its embers were dying now, and she made a mental note to stoke them when she was finished on the phone. They had decided to spend the night at the old house instead of returning to the motel.

"No, she's not here, Bridget. This is what? The fourth time you've called tonight?" Viv's voice came over the cell, making Bridget hungry for home, especially their family's little piece of the historic West Village. She could almost see her parents' high-rise building, and her sister Edie's storefront near Hudson and Perry, where Big Apple Brides was housed. "Really, hon," her mother continued, "it's getting late enough that Granny might have to call you back tomorrow."

Bridget sighed deeply. How could her ancient Granny be in New York such a short amount of time and be busier than Bridget ever was in a month? Before she could say anything, her mother added, "Marley, Cash and Edie took her out to dinner, so Dad and I could…"

"Be alone?" Once more, Bridget felt as if everyone was having a great time tonight except her. It was a feeling that had plagued her throughout her life, largely due to having twins for sisters. Marley and Edie always had each other. And Viv had Joe. Bridget had often felt left to her own devices, and Dermott was the only person who'd really saved her on a consistent basis from that special hell called being a third wheel.

Her mother seemed to read her mind. "How's it going with your buddy?"

Bridget's heart fluttered, and she glanced down at the sexy, nearly see-through white nightie she'd worn to bed. If Dermott wasn't going to talk honestly with her, or sleep with her, she figured the least she could do was torture him if he ever came upstairs. "Long story," she muttered.

"Want to talk about it?"

"Not really. Why don't you tell me news from the front?"

When it came to talking about family, her mother hardly had to be coaxed, and now Bridget listened as her mother rambled. Her dad was busy with a home renovation in the Meat Packing District. Marley and Cash Champagne were still hot and heavy. Even though he owned a club in New Orleans, Cash, who'd just been visiting, was putting off going home, and when he did, he wanted Marley to visit. Bridget had already known Cash's history. It had only recently come out that he was the biological son of Sparky Darden, the hotel empire whiz whose daughter's wedding Edie was now planning. It had turned out that Sparky Darden had hired Edie because he'd worked with their dad, Joe, years ago, and Sparky felt he owed the family an amend. The Bennings' involvement in a snazzy, high-profile wedding was giving all of them new opportunities, and that had brought Marley and Cash into contact.

Otherwise, an announcement about the Hartley House wedding curse had been made on the reality show *Rate the Dates,* and that had cost Edie some business, since people felt a wedding planner should have her own romantic life in order. Allison and Kenneth hadn't canceled, of course. Nor had Julia Darden.

"It's good the Dardens didn't pull out," said Viv.

"Of course they didn't," returned Bridget. "I haven't met Julia, but Marley and Edie say she's really nice. Now, would you please remember to tell Granny to call me when she gets in?"

After her mother promised, Bridget clicked off the phone, then she readjusted the nightie, more artfully arranging the spaghetti straps and tugging down the silk to expose most of her breasts. Making sure the silk edge just touched a nipple, she tilted her head and listened to Dermott moving around downstairs.

He sounded restless. So was she. Somehow, even though they'd been in close proximity all day, she'd managed to avoid him. When they'd searched the property for equipment that would account for the apparitions they'd seen, she'd insisted that he search near the swamps, while she scoured the woods. They'd both been so sure they'd find a projector, a reasonable explanation for what they'd seen. After all, since the sounds had turned out to have come from a movie sound track, then the visual phenomenon must have come from a man-made source.

For hours, she'd combed the murky shoreline of the swamp, her eyes scanning the thick vegetation, just as Dermott had looked inside the house. Just as she was about to give up and go inside to dress for dinner with Garth, Dermott had yelled, telling her to hurry.

"Told you so," he'd said triumphantly when she'd reached one of the upstairs guest rooms. He'd wisked away a cloth and exposed sound recording equipment that was set to a timer.

Bridget had frowned. "Granny's trying to make it seem as if the place is haunted?" she murmured, barely able to believe what she was seeing. Was Granny Ginny haunting her own house? This made no sense, she thought, as Dermott hit the play button. Sounds they'd heard the night before blared in the yard.

"If we follow the sounds, we'll find the trees in which the speakers are hidden," he assured, pointing toward a window.

Moments later, they'd done exactly that. "It looks as if granny's rigged her own place," Bridget said as Dermott pulled down a speaker. "How could she have done this? And why?"

"We'll have to ask her," Dermott said. "And if she's responsible for setting up sound recording equipment then she's also had a hand in the production of the visual apparitions. I'm sure of it."

"I guess we'd better call her," Bridget had said.

But then Granny hadn't been available, so Bridget had excused herself and dressed for dinner at Garth's, and in order to make sure Dermott knew what he was missing, she'd worn the most suggestive outfit she'd packed: fishnets, spike heels and a transparent minidress with a skin-tight underslip. She had no idea how that had affected Dermott— he'd looked totally nonplussed when she'd arrived downstairs—but Garth Cousins had been wowed in a gentlemanly sort of way. They'd talked nonstop during dinner, although she'd decided to withhold the information regarding the recording equipment she and Dermott had found that afternoon. She'd helped Garth with both food preparation and cleanup, so her alone-time with Dermott was further truncated. But now…

Heaving a sigh, Bridget leaned over the side of her grandmother's cushy feather bed, then lifted another stack of yellowed documents into her lap and snuggled against the pillows. Already she'd read from Lavinia's and Marissa's diaries, and as she had, she'd realized Mavis Benchley was right. The papers were so old, threatening to disintegrate, and they belonged someplace safer than the attic, if not the Benchley Library, then some Southern-themed museum. She'd have to talk to Granny about it, as well as ask about the recording equipment upstairs. Slowly, she sifted through the pictures, still wishing she'd found hints as to where the Hartley diamond was hidden, then she returned some photographs to the floor while keeping a handful of pictures. They were made by photographic techniques completely different than those used today, and as she held each up, her blood quickened. She recognized some of the sights, including shots of relatives, probably taken around the nineteen-forties.

"Granny," she whispered, her expression softening as she took in her grandmother, who was around twenty years old and wearing a flattering swimsuit. "And the house." Just looking at Hartley House, she felt strangely breathless. Funny, she thought. Houses aged like people. Just as Granny, the homestead was almost unrecognizable. It was so well-tended, the shell road lined with neatly pruned fruit trees, the now-overgrown drive apparently circular years ago, with a working fountain in the center. Bridget wondered what had become of it, and whether it had been there during the war.

And then she murmured, "Jasper." Said by Granny to be the spitting image of Forrest Hartley, Bridget's biological dad was definitely something to behold. They'd called such men various things over the years: cads, rakes, studs and hunks. Standing in front of a sleek dark horse, Jasper was wearing tight, form-fitting riding pants that left little to the imagination, and he was grinning broadly, a bottle of whiskey in one hand and a burning cigar in the other.

Her heart suddenly skipped a beat. "Yes…" she murmured. What she found next wasn't a photograph, but what looked to be a miniature oil painting in an equally small frame. "It has to be Forrest." Her granny was right. Just like Jasper, the Hartley ancestor had wild blond hair, devilish dark eyes, and judging by the flask at his side, he'd inherited the Hartley gene for loving good whiskey. She shuffled through the pictures more quickly, anxious to find a similar picture of Lavinia.

Suddenly, she startled. Pinpricks lifted the hair at her nape, and she glanced up—half expecting to see Lavinia or Marissa standing in the doorway. But it was Dermott. He'd removed his shirt, and he was standing, framed in the doorway, showing off his L.A. tan, with one long arm extended, his slender fingers curled around the wood of the frame. The hip-hop-style threadbare blue jeans he'd worn to Garth's hung low on his hips, and when she took in the bare inches of flat belly below his navel, her mouth watered. As he padded toward the bed in his stocking feet, a shudder went through her that had absolutely nothing to do with being in a haunted house.

She'd been waiting for him all night. Not that she'd let him know that. Yawning, she glanced back down at the photos in her lap, as if too thoroughly engrossed to give him her full attention, and only when he came to a stop at the foot of the bed did she glance up again, trying to look as bored as he had all day. "Hey," she murmured, making a point of shifting on the covers to better display her long legs. She could only hope he was catching maddening whiffs of the perfume she'd sprayed at her pulse points. "I figured you'd gone to sleep already," she commented without a hint of curiosity.

Eyeing her from the other end of the bed, he looked as if sleep was the last thing on his mind. Seeing desire flash in his eyes only served to increase her own; she was hardly surprised to feel the nearly exposed tips of her breasts tighten. Just as his eyes widened, she stretched her legs again, swung them slowly over the bedside. Rising and heading for the fireplace, she bit back a smile, feeling fairly certain most of her backside was exposed. Bending, she lifted a poker from the rack of fire tools, stirred the fire and returned it.

Turning around, she inhaled sharply. His stocking feet were awfully silent. She hadn't heard him cross the room, and when he stopped in front of her, she enjoyed the thrill surging in her veins. She wasn't about to inquire about their sleeping arrangements tonight, so she lifted an eyebrow and smiled pleasantly, hardly sorry that, with her back to the fire, her breasts had cooled, and were beading once more against silk. His eyes had lighted there, as hot as the fire warming her back. "You should look at the photos," she managed. "There are some small oils, also. They're really interesting."

His eyes were still drifting hungrily down the front of her nightie, and now his lips parted slightly; his tongue appeared, licking at his lips as if they'd gone dry. Intentionally crossing her hands beneath her breasts, trying to communicate a slight annoyance she didn't really feel, she lifted them higher for his perusal, hoping she was driving him crazy with arousal. "I didn't find any pictures of Lavinia, and we already know what Marissa looks like. I did find pictures of Forrest. Even one of my father."

She watched him draw a heaving breath. His eyes were on her legs now. When his gaze shifted, she realized he was looking behind her, into the fire he'd built. Judging from the pulse ticking in his throat, she didn't have to be a rocket scientist to guess what was going on with him. No doubt his heart was starting to race, his veins flooding with whatever energy he was going to need to drag her to bed. But would he?

When he spoke, his voice was rough and husky. "The fire's dying down. Scoot over, and I'll throw another log on it." His eyes found hers. "Unless it's hot enough for you?"

Her hands slid down her sides, landing on her hips, and she drew her shoulders back and tilted her head, as if considering, which meant he could more easily view her affected breasts. "I'm actually a bit chilly in here."

"Looks like it," he said thickly. And then he leaned, caught the nightie's short hem and raised it to expose a white silk triangle of panty. The sides had strings she'd fashioned into bows, and for some strange reason, she wasn't all that surprised when Dermott caught the strings and pulled them.

And then Bridget smiled as her panties hit the floor. "Mission accomplished," she whispered.

She couldn't believe this had taken all day.

7

DERMOTT DRAGGED Bridget to the bed, whispering, "You've been taunting me, Bridge."

"You started it," she murmured when the backs of her knees hit the mattress. The second after she tumbled with him into the soft feathers, the mattress folded around them, enveloping them in warmth. The night chill he'd felt moments ago disappeared, and his eyes narrowed. He studied her as his hands fanned into strands of hair that had flown across a pillow. Those strands had opened as they'd cascaded around her shoulders, looking as soft to him as spreading angel's wings. Silken hanks slid between his splayed fingers now, teasing sensitive flesh and he shivered in response.

"Cold?" she whispered.

"Not now."

"Too bad. I'd warm you up."

"Freezing," he whispered. "I just changed my mind."

She smiled. Her skin looked impossibly soft, glowing and luminescent in the warm firelight, and as he took in the sparkling blue eyes he'd stared into for years, everything seemed to sharpen. When he glanced over his shoulder, it was as if all the outlines in the room—of the furniture, their bodies and the windows—had just been redrawn by an invisible hand wielding a bold black marker.

He blew out a quick sigh, willing himself not to notice how he felt. And yet it was as if he'd been walking through clouds all his life. Just now, he'd stepped from a thick white fog into the blinding clarity of a sunny day. Except, of course, it was really night. And dark and stormy. Outside, just beyond the open lace curtains, the rain was falling hard again, coming in torrents. Just because he knew he'd always been in love with Bridget Benning, and just because he was realizing that with renewed clarity, didn't mean anything else was going to change.

"Think we'll see a haunting tonight?" she whispered.

They'd found the source of the sounds. "Unlikely. Although I've always been haunted by you."

He glanced toward the window. It was almost as loud out there as last night had been, and for a moment, he shut his eyes, the way he often did when he listened to sounds. They seemed rolled into a knotted ball that he took apart, separating each thread: He heard the uneven pant of Bridget's breath, the rustle of fabric even though they were barely moving, the rain slicing sideways, slashing the windowpanes before a boom of thunder rattled the old house to its foundations. He opened his eyes again, just as a flash of lightning bathed the room, then vanished, plunged everything into darkness. She was still smiling at him.

His voice raspy, his mind conscious of how her proximity was affecting his lower body, he said, "Are you afraid the ghosts are coming back?"

"Sure," she murmured lazily. "But you'll protect me." She paused. "Where's Mug?"

"The hallway."

Reaching a hand, he switched off the bedside lamp, wanting to see her lit only by the glow from the fire, and the lightning that appeared in so many different ways: in white bolts, or streaking, dazzling displays of shimmering electricity, or quick, hot flashes that made it seem as if someone had just taken a picture. Each time, it took his eyes a moment to re-adjust to the vision lying beneath him, to the soft contours of Bridget's face, her roundish cheeks and pouting mouth, to the body he could feel trembling against his in anticipation.

His chest felt suddenly tight, and arousal blind-sided him temporarily as her bare legs scissored beneath his while she tried to get comfortable. "You're wrong," he found himself arguing huskily. "I didn't start anything today." Even though he had, of course, by leaving the restaurant and avoiding any talk about their lovemaking. He still had no idea what he wanted to say to her, if anything, although he had no doubt about what he wanted to do.

"Did, too," she countered breathlessly. "And I don't care. Just as long as you finish it."

No problem there. With her panties already gone, he took a splayed hand from the silk of her hair and used it to push up the silk of her nightie, exposing creamy skin. One of his knees fell between her legs, and he covered her breast with a hand. Flexing and releasing his fingers, he slowly massaged the flesh and groaned when he felt a tip constrict. She gasped as he fondled her, and the sound sent pinpricks fanning down his back, further exciting him. Had he really denied himself this all day? They could have been in this bed since this morning, naked and hot and horny, enjoying each other....

Warmth pooled in his belly as he thought of the hours they could have spent, and his groin tingled, his mind filling with images. Before they called it quits, he wanted to see her mouth stretched over his aroused length, her tongue swirling around the head, her hands playing with his balls, feeling their weight in her palms, jostling them while her nails stroked the sacs. And then, just as he was about to come...when he felt unbearably tight...she'd squeeze him ever so gently, making him explode...

He wanted to bind her wrists and ankles to the four high posts of the bed, too, and watch her twist as if to escape the silk that kept her captive. She'd be just as excited as he, though, her legs spread impossibly wide, so her feminine folds were visible, ready for the slow finger he saw himself sliding between them. He'd hold open the folds, and she'd gasp, her dampness slick on his fingers as the pad of his thumb would settle on the nub of her clitoris. Pressuring it, he'd begin to rub.

Just the thoughts made him suck in an edgy breath. He was aching, barely able to believe he was going to be inside Bridget again. That nightie had done the trick. When he'd seen the peachy edges of her relaxed nipples and her ridiculously taunting smile, he'd wanted to make her remember the lesson she'd learned last night, that he could pleasure her better than any other man.

Yes. Just like before, he'd make her scream, willing her to take more pleasure. Reaching with a free hand, he unsnapped his pants, muttering in frustration as he raked the zipper over his hard-on. Just when he thought the zipper had caught, he winced, but it gave and slid all the way down. As it came to rest in a fold of denim, the packed heat encased in briefs spilled through the open V. He backed from the bed, just enough to push the denim and briefs down.

All the while, Bridget stroked him with her gaze. She looked almost startled, surveying his burning desire. Yes, he was painfully aroused. So much so that he cried out when she sat and reached for him, looking for all the world like a kid wanting candy. When she fisted him, his head reeled back and his knees buckled and hit the mattress. His eyes shut as her slender fingers started to slide.

Vaguely, he knew he had to push away her hand. He'd never last. But he waited another second, letting her circle her thumb under the head. His mind disintegrated into cinders and ash, and his body flooded with heat as her hands milked him, daring him to come now. He wanted to…

But he reached down, fighting with the fingers wrapped around an engorged length she'd left throbbing; slowly, he pried them off, then he lay on top of her again, his kneecap suddenly touched by wetness, her dampness and heat.

"You left me in the restaurant this morning," she muttered, lifting her hands high above her head, urging him to remove her nightie, which he did. "You didn't want to have sex with me."

"Well, I do now."

Not wanting to further explain himself—he didn't even know if he could—he covered her mouth with his to cut short the small talk, his blood pulsing through him with gulping thuds that warmed him to his toes. The feel of her mouth on his—warm and sweet, with the lips open and trembling—urged him on. He reached between her legs, testing her dampness with a finger, then thrust inside her, his mind blanking as his length sank deep into dark velvet. His neck craned instinctively, his head arching back. What was she doing to him? Was he going to lose his head over her? Maybe he already had. He'd forgotten to use a condom—he didn't even know if she had any more of them—and he sure hadn't brought any, never thinking…

But here they were. In bed. And he realized something else—that she must not care, since she'd have stopped him. It had been years since he'd felt this kind of connection, flesh on flesh. Heat twirled inside him as his mouth found hers again, this time slamming down hard, drinking in more of a kiss that was urging him to oblivion as he pushed deeper.

Her fingers were sticky, damp and clammy when they found his hips, and they shouldn't have felt sexy, but the touch shoved him to the edge. He withdrew, her body tightening around his, then thrust once more. She was getting slicker, hotter, and his mind reeled anew each time her damp curls met his.

"Bridge," he whispered, his voice barely audible. After all these years, was he really loving her? A hand glided on her ribs, skating over each bone, then stopping under a breast and stroking the side until she was muttering. He was no longer capable of kissing her, only thrusting harder, his finger and thumb rubbing a taut nub of a nipple until she uttered a low chortling gasp. He went taut. He was going to explode.

He'd wanted her so long. Dreamed of this. All day, he'd tried to keep his hands off her, knowing this could go nowhere. It was just a whim for her. He'd only get hurt. He'd heard the dismissive way she answered people in town who'd assumed they were a couple. Damn it, she'd get her fill and back off soon enough. She did with every man who tried to get close. He'd watched her do it for years. She was flighty, indecisive, impulsive...

Huskily, he muttered, "I want to make you as crazy as you make me."

She was breathless. "I make you crazy?"

It was infuriating. What did she think? She'd been standing in front of the fire in a scrap of fabric through which he could make out every contour—the breasts and nipples, a flat tummy and the nip of a waist. Her panties had been showing, and she'd exposed those slender legs that she was now wrapping around his back, using them to pull him deeper....

His mouth lathered wet kisses from the bud of a breast to her neck before he bit her ear and whispered, "Really crazy."

Using his cheeks to suction her deep inside his mouth, his own flesh quivered when the fiery tip of his tongue sizzled on an impossibly hard nipple. For a second, his mind spun into pure crystal darkness, and he thought that no woman could make a man feel this way. This was too good. Too perfect.

Stretching his lips, he devoured her mouth now. Slowly, he glided his hands around her back and downward, and she flinched in pleasure when he cupped the warm flesh of her bare backside. Suddenly, he jerked her upward, soliciting a gasp of ecstacy as he slammed deeper. She tried to arch, but he controlled her movements, leaving her powerless to do anything but lie back and enjoy. He went taut again. He wanted to hold on. Had to. He could wait until the whole world exploded inside her, shattering. It was his revenge for how she'd taunted him all day, all his life, really....

He'd vowed he wouldn't come to bed tonight.

But he had. And it was worth this pleasure, worth any pain that was to follow. Worth losing Carrie Masterson. And worth being laughed out of town by everyone in their social circle who had known for years he was too smitten to say no to Bridget Benning. He was still hanging by a thread. Seeing red, then black. He thrust deeper. Deeper. How was that even possible? He thought vaguely.

Damn. Damn. Damn. The word was a mantra in his mind now.

She made him feel weak, emotionally. But powerful, too, because she was so wet and warm. He tightened his muscles once more, wanting to feel her come first, waiting for her to convulse, but it was no use. The orgasm took him.

"Sorry," he muttered forcefully, barely able to speak as spasms shook him. She didn't seem to hear. Her arms and legs squeezed, and she rocked against him, rolling on the curve of her spine, crying with release.

"I guess that was a quickie," he whispered breathlessly a moment later, his weight collapsing on top of her.

"Kiss me while you recover," Bridget whispered back, her breath still coming in pants, tasting salty on his mouth, her hands in his damp hair now, her soft fingertips gathering the dew of perspiration from his neck before she thrust them deeply into the strands, grabbing them in fistfuls. "Kiss me while you recover, Derm," she repeated. "And then we'll move on, from the quickie to the long-ee."

Rolling to his back and taking her with him, drawing her into his arms, he jerked covers out from under them, and then pulled them over her back, tucking her in. "I just need a quick nap," he promised. "Ten minutes."

She considered. "Five."

BRIDGET INHALED DEEPLY, smelling Southern scents that were thick and sensual, foreign yet alluring. No…enticing. That was the word. Better yet, seductive. She imagined trailing wisteria creeping along branches of cedars hung with moss. Farther away, down by the swamp, the dark, murky waters stirred with a brisk wind, churning in choppy waves, choking up mud and lichens.

"What in thunder's wrong with you? Can't you hear me, Missy?"

Bridget tried to blink, but her eyes were too heavy to open. She was tired, her body spent from lovemaking, and yet urgency raced in her blood. She had to wake up! She had to listen! Something important was happening! But what? And she was supposed to listen to...whom?

"Bridget! Get up now. Your granny's up north, and you girls are well past the age of marriage. Old maids. Spinsters. Lawdy, how could you have done such a thing as having relations with that man? And in your already compromised position—by which I mean you're cursed, if you've forgotten!"

Once more, Bridget tried to blink, but she merely turned restlessly in bed, her mind whirling. She was trying to sleep, she was so very tired, but a voice in her mind just wouldn't let her.

Suddenly, she gasped. She wasn't in bed at all! She was downstairs in her granny's house, walking barefoot through the darkened rooms, her anxious fingers combing the walls, looking for electric light switches but they were no longer here. They were gone! There was light, though, coming from far off, and as she approached, it brightened, shining through a doorway as if beckoning her.

Her lips parted as she reached the threshold of the lit room. Of course. The parlor. She should have known. But it wasn't the parlor of today. The green fringed rug was gone, as well as the oil lamps that had been wired for electricity. Candles in the chandelier were lit now, seemingly hundreds of them. Startled by the beauty of the fixture, Bridget barely noticed that she'd crossed the threshold, her feet moving as if of their own accord, her eyes widening as she took in the flickering tongues of flame. There couldn't have been hundreds, not really, but every ray was magnified a hundred-fold by the prisms, sending glimmers of rainbow light to the walls and ceiling.

"Beautiful," she whispered, thinking she wanted to be married right here, in this very room. But who…

Just as she thought of Dermott, she heard fast, short, stacatto footsteps on the hardwood. They were coming from the room behind her, and fast approaching. Only when she whirled and pressed her hand to her chest, to still her beating heart, did she realize she wasn't wearing her nightie, after all, as she'd assumed, but rather, a long, flowing muslin gown that looked as if it belonged to another century. And footsteps were still coming, heading right toward her!

A tall, slender woman suddenly stepped over the threshold. She was beautiful, with dark, almond-shaped eyes, high cheekbones, and thick sensual lips; her skin was the same color as the kerchief she wore, a reddish chestnut that deepened under the light. Bridget watched as the woman put her hands on the hips of a crisp dark dress, which was covered by a white apron. Pursing her lips in censure, she gave Bridget a once-over. "Glad to see you put something on," she muttered. "I just hate talking to people in their dreams when they're naked. You'd be amazed at how many people don't dress decently for bed."

Bridget could only stare. "What?"

"Oh, never you mind," said the woman with a frustrated sigh. "The important thing is that you're here, regardless of what you're wearing. Now, I take it you've heard of the curse?"

Bridget's heart missed a beat. She was starting to panic. Had the ghosts come back? Was this a dream? Or was this really happening? Had she sleepwalked down to the parlor, only to meet Lavinia Delroy? And where had she gotten this strange muslin gown? It looked like something Marissa would have worn. "Uh…" Her voice stuck in her throat. She cleared it. And when that didn't work, she cleared it again. "Uh…are you Lavinia?"

The woman stared back at her for a very long moment. "Who else would I be?"

So it was. "You came to…give me advice?"

Lavinia's lips parted. She shook her head and rolled her eyes, heaved a great sigh and said, "Why else would I come from the grave and appear in a dream? You certainly are dense. What do you think I came for? To trade recipes?"

"Of course not," Bridget said, thinking this was the strangest conversation she'd ever had, regardless if it came from this world or the next.

"I'm pretty sure I figured out where Miss Marissa hid the ring," Lavinia said quickly. "She won't tell me because she's still madder'n a hornet about dying during the war, and, of course, she still wants everyone on earth to suffer for it.

"If she can't be happy, Miss Marissa's the type to take everyone down with her, if you know what I mean. The world's full of people such as that. Now, mind you, she's got her good qualities, but charity toward others was never one of them. Anyhow, regarding that ring, my usual powers of prophecy have failed me time and time again. Still, like I say, I think I know where she might have put it now. And I need your help, Bridget. Help, which you'll want to give, of course, since you and your sisters will benefit from the lifting of the curse. Trouble is, I can't get to the ring, by myself. You see—" Pausing, Lavinia raised her arm and swiped it toward the chandelier.

Bridget gasped.

But the hand went right through all the delicate crystals. "See," explained Lavinia. "When it comes to certain tasks, I'm limited. Handicapped, as they say in your time. So, what I need for you to do for me is…"

A boom sounded, and Bridget startled. It was the worst possible moment to be wrenched from the dream. The ring had been right there. Right within her grasp! Lavinia was going to save the day. Remove the curse. Groggily, Bridget tried to blink— and this time, she was successful. Batting her eyes, she realized Dermott's warm body was next to hers, and while, she'd thought she was still wearing the muslin gown, she now realized she was naked.

"Bridge," Dermott's voice was so husky that they could have been making love. He shook her shoulder hard. "Bridge. Wake up." He was speaking in such hushed tones that something must be wrong.

She glanced up, her eyes opening in slits. "What?"

His gaze slid slowly toward the foot of the bed. When Bridget's followed, her heart missed a beat. She scooted upward instinctively, pulling covers with her to shield her breasts, and then she blinked once more. But the apparition at the foot of the bed didn't budge. "Marissa," she whispered.

The other woman was merely standing there, wearing her wedding gown. Fortunately, there was no blood on it. She was unearthly in her beauty, her skin flawless and pale, her eyes sparkling blue. The colors of her face and dress wavered, making her look as if she was lying in a lake, covered by rippling waters. Through her transparent form, Bridget could make out objects on the other side of her—the old chest of drawers and antique chamber pot. Vaguely aware that one of Dermott's long arms had wrapped around her back, gathering her close, Bridget could only stare as Miss Marissa lifted her left hand to show the fingers, drawing attention to the fact that she was no longer wearing her ring.

Was she still dreaming? Bridget wondered. But no. She didn't think so. She glanced at Dermott. He was naked. Sleepy-looking. Yes, it seemed as if this was reality.

Or at least as real as reality could get when ghosts were visiting it. Deciding to go with the flow of what seemed to be happening, Bridget forced herself to mask her fear and mustered her sternest possible voice, imitating Lavinia, who she figured might be one of the few people on earth—or in heaven or hell, as it were—who Miss Marissa actually listened to.

"Now, you look here, Miss Marissa," she began, "you're just trying to get me to stop talking to Lavinia because she wants to help me end the curse. That's why you're interrupting my dreams." As soon as the words were out, she realized that, while they had absolutely no affect on the apparition in front of her, it certainly felt good to blow off a little steam. After all, this was the woman who'd been ruining her love life for years, right? And only moments ago, she'd had to put up with Lavinia, who was a bit of a nag.

"I heard you were spoiled rotten, Miss Marissa," she continued. "And Lavinia's not the only one who thinks so. Granny Ginny says the same thing," Bridget forced herself to continue, shuddering. "You ruin her sleep, night after night. And what kind of woman would destroy the love lives of other young women years after her own ended? Do you know what it's like to go on hundreds of bad dates? How it knocks down a young woman's self-esteem? Ghost or no ghost, you're a spiteful thing, aren't you, Marissa?"

Suddenly, Bridget really couldn't take the whole situation, anymore. She grabbed the covers and despite the fear coursing through her, she leaped out of bed. "Do you really want to ruin everyone else's life? Are you really that selfish?" Bridget headed for the foot of the bed, but as soon as she reached it and stretched out her hand, the apparition vanished.

And then she realized the house was stone silent.

She tilted her head. No lightning. No thunder. No footsteps. The rain had stopped. "Dermott," she muttered. "Turn on the light."

He flicked on the light, and that's when she realized this really wasn't a dream. When she turned toward him, he looked lusciously alive, albeit as white as a ghost. She swallowed hard. "Can you believe this?" she asked.

"There's got to be an explanation," he muttered

shakily as she rushed toward the pile of pictures she'd left on the floor beside the bed, the wood feeling cold on her bare feet. Wrapping herself in the sheet she carried around her, she squatted in front of the stack, her hands quickly riffling through them, her eyes moving between the pictures and Dermott.

"There was a miniature of Forrest," she explained. "So maybe there's one of Lavinia. I was just starting to go through all these when…" *You came in and we made love.* Pausing, she stared into Dermott's eyes, hers glazing with heat, then she quickly continued, her hands moving rapidly as she sorted the artifacts. "There's just got to be one."

"Bridge." Dermott was still in bed, and now he slowly sat up, bunching pillows behind him. "Did you just see that, too?" he murmured, stunned.

"Yeah," she said, looking at him. "But it's okay. I don't think they mean us any harm."

"You can't believe…" His voice trailed off. "I mean, I know we didn't find any equipment that could produce images like those we saw today, but we did establish that Garth wants the timber and Mavis holds a grudge, not just because of the Hartley-Benchley history, but because of Garth. And I still think there must be…"

Projectors in the trees that would account for what we're seeing. "Here," she murmured, suddenly lifting a small oil miniature in an ornate gold frame. Her lips parted in stunned glee as she took in the stately woman in the picture, a red-skinned woman with high cheekbones, almond-shaped eyes, and thick sensual lips. Definitely, she'd never seen this woman, except in her dreams. There was no portrait of her in the parlor, as there was of Miss Marissa. She'd appeared in Bridget's mind, nonetheless, looking exactly like the woman in this portrait. Holding it up, so Dermott could see, she whispered, "Lavinia. This proves she exists. That *ghosts* exist," she clarified.

And then she set the picture aside and lunged into Dermott's arms, shivering but happy. Quickly, she caught him up on what had just happened in her dream, trying to recount for him every single word Lavinia had said, not that Dermott would ever believe in ghosts. He was too pragmatic. Still, he held her and listened, and she could tell by the light in his eyes that he, too, was starting to hope that all this was true, after all, even if he didn't really believe it. This meant Lavinia might appear again. And next time, maybe she'd show Bridget the exact location of the ring. If she did so, maybe Bridget would be released from the curse, and she and Dermott could...

"Let's make love again," he whispered, when she was finished recounting her dream.

She had a moment's hesitation. "Don't you feel watched now?"

Sending her a long look, he said, "I still believe we'll find some kind of light-show mechanisms out here tomorrow. Just like we found recording equipment. Which is probably why your grandmother hasn't called you back yet. She's avoiding the confrontation she'll have with you when you tell her we discovered her 'ghosts' are the *Gone with the Wind* sound track, and that the recording equipment is set up in her own house."

"But just now…"

"Miss Marissa wasn't real," assured Dermott. "And even if she was," he added, pulling her into his arms and against his growing erection, "we're not going to do anything centuries-old ghosts haven't seen before."

Bridget couldn't help but chuckle wickedly. "I wouldn't count on that, Dermott Brandt."

8

"CELL PHONE," Bridget whispered raspily when a blaring version of the *Exorcist* theme filled the room. They'd jokingly programmed their phones to the song.

Dermott didn't open his eyes. "Yours or mine?"

"Dunno."

He chuckled softly. "Should we toss a coin for which one of us is going to open our eyes first?"

Bridget giggled, then suddenly sobered. First, she thought of Marissa, and how frightening it would be to see her again. And then, she wondered if Carrie Masterson was calling again. If so, should Bridget answer Dermott's phone? No...she could never do that. Still, maybe if Carrie realized that Bridget and Dermott were in bed, she'd back off. *Doubtful,* Bridget decided. Who was she kidding? Sighing, she considered trying to ask Dermott about his relationship again. But how? So far, he hadn't exactly been receptive to her wheedling.

This was the kind of thing Bridget hated most about contemporary romance. Or actually, she mentally amended, maybe romance had been this way for centuries. Granny and Mavis had certainly both wanted Garth. And if Miss Marissa couldn't have

Forrest, she wanted everyone else to suffer for all eternity.

Blowing out another sigh as her mind whirled with too many thoughts, Bridget said, "Well, this is what we get for programming to the same ringer." They'd done so many other things together, too, hadn't they? Bought the same T-shirts, used the same hair and skin products, usually shopping together for them on Saturdays in Chinatown. Sliding a hand down his side as she rolled away from the warmth of his body, she reached over the bedside, to the stack of pictures still on the floor. Using a finger, she stirred the sundries on top—nightie, jeans, wallet, coins…

"Mine," she finally announced. Sighing, she stretched her body against Dermott's as she lifted the phone, unable to believe the astonishing physical electricity they generated together. Even better, she could tell Dermott was half-aroused, ready to go once more. "We must have banished the ghosts," she whispered, staring at the call number and seeing it was her mother's. "All the electricity we generated last night must have blown all the fuses in the house, so to speak." They'd heard no strange noises at all, and seen no apparitions after Miss Marissa had vanished.

"That, or the ghosts decided to give us some privacy."

"Do I detect some irony in your tone? You say that as if you believe ghosts don't exist."

"What say we agree to disagree on this issue," murmured Dermott, pulling her into his arms and running his fingers through her hair. "Meantime, no offense but I'm getting tired of hearing the cell phone.

Why don't you do me a favor and answer your phone?"

Yawning, she flipped it open. "Hello?" Hearing the voice on the other end, she rapidly blinked and scooted upward in bed. "Granny?"

"Sorry to call so early, Miss Bridget," drawled her granny in a voice so sugary that it could have distilled lemons, "but your sisters took me out to dinner last night, along with Marley's new beau, Cash Champagne, so I just now got your VM."

Bridget squinted. "VM?"

There was a long pause. "Uh…that's voice mail, precious. Surely, you've heard of it, since you have the feature in your own telephone."

Bridget awakened another notch. "Sure," she said. "I just usually call it voice mail, not VM. Sorry, but I'm a little groggy. I'm just now waking up."

Granny chortled, and Bridget heard the sound of her hand covering a phone receiver. "She just woke up," she called, presumably to Bridget's mother or father. Lowering her voice, she said, "How are you supposed to find that ring if you're in a bed all day, Miss Bridget? Answer me that! And while I hate to pry, I can hear someone else, which means you're occupying yourself in ways an unmarried girl shouldn't."

Bridget was half-tempted, of course, to bring up Garth Cousins. Realizing she wasn't thinking clearly enough to deal with her grandmother yet, she glanced toward a travel alarm on the bedside table. Feeling something strikingly similar to the jolt that a Starbucks latte might have given her, she further straightened her shoulders. "Eleven," she murmured. Granny was right. She and Dermott had slept away half the day! A slow smile curled her lips as memories flooded her. Of course, that was only because they'd been up all night. Her insides felt gloriously mushy, and her skin was tingling all over. She felt almost too good to ruin the mood by confronting her wily grandmother.

But then, she had no other choice. "We talked to Garth and Mavis," she began, not bothering to hide her pique, although it was mitigated by the slow circles Dermott was starting to draw on her bare thigh. "In fact, we even had dinner with Garth. And it was Mavis who told me where to find the old pictures and diaries in the attic. Why didn't you tell me about them, Granny? How was I supposed to find the ring under these circumstances? You didn't even tell me the real reason why you and Mavis—"

"That's not why you're really calling," Granny Ginny cut in, her tone soliciting a loud sigh of annoyance from Bridget, who glanced through the open lace curtains onto another gray day. A light rain was falling, just a drizzle, that Bridget suddenly fancied might be Miss Marissa's tears as she cried for her long-lost love.

"It's not?" she muttered.

"Nope," announced Granny. "I already talked to your mother, and she said you found the recording equipment I set up in one of the old guest rooms." Suddenly, Granny Ginny's voice broke. "I'm so sorry, you dear child," she crooned. "I didn't mean to send you barking up any wrong trees. But well, you see..."

When her anguished voice broke off, Bridget found herself softening against her will. Her grandmother could be the world's worst manipulator, but right now, she sounded very sincere. "I'm waiting," Bridget said.

"There really are ghosts in my house," Granny Ginny rushed on. "You've got to believe me. Anybody in Big Swamp will back me up on it. But they'd gone quiet, lately. Oh, I'd hear them, but only once a month or so. And I started to worry. After all, they're our only real hope for finding the ring and ending the curse. Probably Marissa knows where it is, and what other clues do we have? Contrary to anything Mavis Benchley might have said, I've pored over those old diaries and pictures, myself, looking for answers."

"And so you decided to rig your own house with a sound system?"

"Yes, honey. But that's all I did. I just hoped to get people interested in the place again. In fact, I was thinking that I might try to open a bed and breakfast there, and that the ghosts might be a draw. I can make money that way, and then Garth won't try to strong-arm me into cutting down the trees. Anyway, this was the only way to make sure you'd be interested and go down there and find the ring. When I showed up in New York, and saw the exact replica of the ring on your finger, I knew I'd done the right thing."

Bridget thought about the past couple of days. "What about the apparitions?"

Granny Ginny's voice quickened. "You actually saw something?" She paused. "In the house?"

Bridget considered. If Granny was responsible

for the light projections, as she was for the recorded sounds, she was never going to admit it. "It's a long story," she decided to say. "I'll tell you when we get back."

"Get back?"

"Kenneth and Allison's wedding is coming up soon."

"Your sister, Edie's, running around like a chicken with her head cut off, finalizing all the plans. And in the middle of it, she's got plenty going on with that high-society wedding for the Dardens, too. But promise me you won't come back until you find the ring, Miss Bridget. You're our last hope. If you don't find it, you girls will always be cursed, and Marley and Cash look so cute together! I'd just hate for them to have to break up!"

Feeling uneasy, Bridget glanced at Dermott. He looked absolutely scrumptious, lying on his back naked, with a hand nestled in his chest hairs. She'd never felt more sure she wanted the curse lifted, if there really was one. "I'd better go," she managed, not wanting to get into another circular conversation with her granny. Hanging up, she said, "Granny still maintains I've got to find the ring. And she swears she didn't put any light equipment on the property, only the reel-to-reel."

She paused, wondering how, under these circumstances, she was supposed to continue the search. Granny had already combed the diaries for clues, which was to have been Bridget's next move. And now she was wide-awake, so she couldn't go back to sleep and hope Lavinia would just happen to insert herself into her dream again. "We could have a seance," she suddenly suggested, feeling her spirits rise.

Dermott didn't look particularly thrilled by the idea. Always one to bring up movie references, since movies were his business, he said, "Remember what happened when they used that Ouija board in the *Exorcist*."

Sending her eyes heavenward, she rolled on top of him, placed her clasped hands on his chest, and smiled into his eyes. "True. All hell broke loose. But you don't even believe in ghosts, right?"

His hands circled her neck, and he used his fingertips to pressure her nape, to draw her mouth to his. Only after he'd kissed her deeply, thoroughly plundering, did he say, "Yeah. But let's just say I don't like to tempt fate."

His skin beneath hers was tantalizingly warm, so she slid a flattened palm down his side, shifting her weight just enough that she could place it between them. A thrill shot to her core as she stroked him intimately, loving how his eyes widened and his lips parted, the audible intake of breath. "Just what *do* you want to do?" she murmured.

"Well, I guess we ought to search the property some more, to see if we find any light projectors. I don't believe your grandmother."

"Hmm." She kept touching him. "And?"

"That's about it," he said, his voice sounding positively shivery with what she was doing to him. "Kenneth and Allison's wedding really is in a couple of days. We can't risk not making it back, since we're in it."

"We've got plenty of time."

"I want a couple of days' padding, in case the car breaks down or something. Could you imagine getting married and having your attendants not show?"

Her heart missed a beat. And for just a second, she found herself imagining getting married—to Dermott. "No. Besides, we might have to stop at a little seaside resort," she murmured, her eyes still shut, her fingers massaging him. "And what other activities can you think of, to help us occupy our time today," she whispered suggestively.

"It seems like you've come up with a good idea, Bridge."

Laughing softly, she shifted her weight once more, now lying beside him. Skating her fingers across his chest and shutting her eyes tightly, she murmured in a voice she hoped approximated that of a medium, "We are communicating with the body of Dermott Brandt. Will Dermott Brandt please come out…" Her fingers skated lower on his ribs, and she felt his skin flinch at her touch on his lower belly. "Or up," she added with a giggle as her fingers traveled around his growing erection, twining in the curling hairs. Scooting downward, she used the heel of her palm to capture the root of him, and then, with firm pressure, glided her fingers over the whole length, pressing it hard to his belly.

Power surged through her when she glanced at his face. Already he was lost to the newfound ecstacy they were enjoying together. "You don't look nearly aroused enough," she suddenly whispered huskily.

And then she leaned and lowered her mouth to his flesh.

"CELL PHONE," Bridget murmured again many hours later, as the *Exorcist* theme song blared, interrupting her sleep. Blinking her eyes open, she felt a sense of déjà vu even as she spoke. "Dermott?" He didn't answer. For a second, she was sure she was still dreaming, but when she rolled over, pulling the covers with her, she realized she wasn't. This was reality, and Dermott was no longer beside her.

He'd been in the room, though, and judging by the looks of things, recently. Hmm, she thought. Judging by the smells, as well. She smiled. She and Dermott had always loved to cook together, and now the heady scents of garlic, basil and peppers were wafting upstairs. He must have decided to let her sleep while he cooked the food they'd bought in Big Swamp the night they'd arrived.

"And coffee," she murmured. Fisting her hand, she drew it inward, toward her body and whispered. "Yes." It was as if Dermott was reading her mind. Right about now, she could almost taste the java. From the scent, she'd bet he was preparing a pot of spiced chicory coffee from a special blend Garth Cousins had insisted they take home. Her smile broadened. Garth had been quite a character, full of stories about Big Swamp, definitely a good match for her grandmother. She chuckled. Who knew what the troubles had been in Mavis and Garth's marriage, but Bridget suspected Mavis's continued interest in Garth had less to do with Garth himself, and more to do with the fact that her arch-rival, Ginny Hartley, had wound up with him.

Her smile broadening, Bridget sighed deeply.

What a day! Maybe, just maybe, it was the very best of her life. Squeezing her eyes shut, she tried to think back to days she might have liked as well as this one. She'd spent an incredible day on Coney Island once, another in Bay Ridge, and yet another on a film-location shoot in Denver. Suddenly, she acknowledged the common thread. Each day had been spent with Dermott. While working on a film sound track, he'd pretended she was his girlfriend, so a studio would pay for the Denver trip, and although she'd hated flying even before 9/11, she'd done so, anyway, taking plenty of kava kava to calm her nerves. They'd had a blast, driving over to Boulder for lunch, looking at a world populated by moose, horses and mountains, everything so different from their home turf. But today was the very best of all.

They'd never searched the property, and Dermott had talked her out of holding a seance anywhere but on the Ouija board of his body, which meant they'd stayed in bed all day, making love. Never dressing, they'd stopped only for trips to the kitchen, bringing up coffee, bowls of fruit and leftovers from Garth.

When the ringing stopped and the phone shifted into voice mail, Bridget relaxed. She'd call back later. Or Dermott could, if the call had been for him. She just hoped it wasn't Carrie, not that Dermott could still be interested in her, given what was happening between them. "Amazing," she whispered, staring through the open curtains. She'd been so preoccupied that she hadn't even thought to turn off the ringers.

Stretching, she glanced around. The room was cool, a draft from the February evening seeping in through creaky floorboards and cracked window moldings. It was almost dark, too, full of shifting shadows, and when she peered into the room's corners, they were barely visible now. "Perfect for hiding ghosts," she whispered.

Lifting her voice, she ventured, "C'mon, Lavinia. Dermott doesn't even believe in you, but I do. Why don't you drop me a line and tell me where the ring is? Maybe you could draw a map in the dust on this furniture." Before they left, she decided that she and Dermott really needed to do a bit of cleaning for her granny.

She glanced toward the fire that Dermott had built before he'd gone downstairs, saw the still-burning kindling under the logs, and reasoned he hadn't been gone long. As she watched flames lick the wood, she felt mesmerized by the soft snapping sounds and the sparks spiraling. The fire was slowly taking off the room's chill, she realized.

Not that it mattered. Dermott's body had kept her warmer than a thousand fires, and besides, she'd never minded cold weather, nor rain. She loved extremes—storms and high winds—since she loved to snuggle, and Granny's bed was the perfect place for it. As she hunkered in the soft feathers and down pillows, she felt positively delicious.

Outside, the day was long gone, but night hadn't fallen yet, either. Through the window, she could see a deep, eerie twilight. The rain had stopped, and the sky seemed to have cracked apart. Rays of pink and purple shot through gray-tinged puffy clouds that looked like billowing smoke, exposing surreal patches of midnight-blue. Pearly white stuff rolled like the cotton once grown on Hartley land. Shimmering pink undersides gleamed through the white, looking almost identical to the incandescent insides of the broken shells lining the driveway. It was the kind of sky one rarely saw in the city, and mostly Bridget associated it with paintings by Titian, which she'd seen in the Met.

"But it's all real," she whispered. Her. Dermott. Their lovemaking. The ghosts. Everything. She shivered with delight. Probably Lavinia had been trying to access her consciousness the whole time she'd been asleep, but Dermott had worn her out, so Bridget couldn't have heard a thing, not even a determined ghost.

She heaved another sigh when the *Exorcist* blared once more. "Who is it?" she muttered, rebelling against the interruption, but leaning over the bedside this time, nevertheless, to fish for the phones. Probably Granny, she assumed, calling to see if she and Dermott had found the ring. Grabbing the ringing phone, she flipped it open, and when she spoke, the sound of her own voice startled her, since it was octaves deeper, husky with lovemaking. "Hello?"

There was a long pause, then a very snotty-sounding, "Bridget?"

She held the phone out a fraction, just enough to identify the phone as Dermott's. Not that she hadn't known the second she'd heard Carrie Masterson's voice. Hmm, she thought. It might as well have been Linda Blair calling. Too bad she and Dermott had been together when they'd bought their phones, also.

They were identical except for the color of the cases, and it was too dark in the room to tell them apart.

She made the snap decision not to give an inch, and to sound as if she had no idea who this was. Yes, she wasn't at all proud of it, but she'd make it sound as if women other than Carrie Masterson called Dermott all day. "I'm sorry. He's not here right now. May I ask who's calling?" She was hardly proud of the deception, and she wished with all her heart that she could find some reasonable reason to keep Dermott from this woman—other than the fact that she wanted him for herself, of course.

"It's Carrie," Carrie said. "Is he…?"

Bridget simply couldn't interrupt all this perfection by taking the phone downstairs. This day belonged to her and Dermott. "He's unavailable at the moment, but I'll tell him you called." Hearing skittering in the hallway, Bridget glanced up just as Mug charged into the room. Something dark wiggled between his clenched teeth, and before Bridget could identify the object, he lunged onto the bed, his dripping paws tracking across Granny Ginny's butter-yellow spread and white sheets. Bridget squealing, jumped to her feet and shouted, "Mug!" Then she covered the space over her heart with her hand. "A stick," she muttered, now realizing she was standing on the bed, stark naked and clutching the phone. "Mug's got a stick in his mouth," she managed. "I thought it was…I don't know, a mouse or something. Something living. Look, I'm really sorry, but he just jumped onto the bed, and his paws are muddy, so I'd better—"

"You're in bed?" Carrie exploded.

Given the time of day, Bridget realized that didn't look good. She leaned again, reached into her bag and grabbed a sundress, vaguely feeling exposed and wanting to cover herself, even though Carrie Masterson couldn't really see her, of course.

Letting go of the phone long enough to pull the dress over her head, she said, "Uh...yeah." She started to say she could explain everything, but why on earth should she explain anything at all to Carrie Masterson? Besides, Carrie's suspicions were absolutely correct. A sudden surge of anger went through her. Who was this woman, anyway? Bridget only knew her superficially, and she had no idea what her relationship was to Dermott. Nor had Dermott told her. And he should have, Bridget decided. Had they slept together? Suddenly, she had to know. Taking a deep breath, she said, "I'd better go. I'll have Dermott call you."

"I can't believe this," Carrie muttered. "You're in bed with him, aren't you?"

Bridget couldn't believe this, either. And she definitely didn't like Carrie's tone. "What if I am?"

Carrie uttered a sound of protest. "You're so selfish," she rushed on. "You get in the way of every woman who even thinks they'd like to get to know Dermott. And you know what? He was sick of it, too. He's tired of you hanging around when you're not even his girlfriend. He promised me he was going down there with you for only one reason, to end your friendship."

Impossible. "You're crazy," Bridget said. "Dermott would never do that."

"Oh, no? Why don't you ask him? Unless he didn't

see you at all, he knew he could never break the hold you have on him. So, he was going to tell you. He's a fine man. Good company. He loves his career, and he's worked on a lot of different areas of his life, too. He wants kids, a family, a home. And he knows you can't give any of that to him." Carried uttered another sound of disgust. "What?" she demanded. "Did you finally seduce him for a little sex? Is that all you care about? Other women want to try to make a life with him. To give him a home. But you're holding him back. Women leave because you always show up, get in the way, and make demands on him, without every really giving him anything—"

"I've heard enough," Bridget managed to interject. But she was frozen, her chest tight, her hands clutching the phone. She felt as if she'd just been sucker punched and all the air had been sucked from her body. "Dermott wasn't going to end our friendship," she repeated in defense.

But when she glanced up, Dermott was standing in the doorway, and he said, "Yes, I was."

9

NUMBLY, Bridget flipped the phone shut, hardly caring that she'd hung up on Carrie. Just as she tossed it to the bed, Mug curled at her feet, shivering from the rainy night, oblivious to the tension in the room and gnawing his new stick. Barely able to believe what Dermott had said, Bridget gingerly got off the bed. The wood floor felt cold on her feet, sending a shiver through her body, and she was glad when a log in the fireplace caught, a brief flare of flame better illuminating the room.

Edging toward the fire, seeking its warmth, she kept her eyes on Dermott. He was shirtless, having pulled on his pants for the trip downstairs, and he was carrying a tray laden with steaming leftovers from Garth's, as well as the bottle of whiskey they'd nipped from on the night of their arrival. Presumably he'd brought the leftovers since the sauce would take a few more hours. He'd figured she'd wake up hungry.

Which she had. But it didn't matter now. At the moment, her whole world had spun on its axis. She watched as Dermott glanced around and realized all the tabletops were covered with objects. Leaning, he set the tray on the floor, then started toward her, but she held out a staying hand.

"Carrie said you only came to Florida with me to tell me you didn't want to be my friend." She tried to fight it, but her voice rose with panic. "My *friend*," she repeated. "Were you going to refuse to see me anymore? At *all*? Just—" She opened her hands, inviting an explanation. "Wham bam—and no more contact?"

He stopped in front of her. She couldn't see where his pupils ended and the irises of his eyes began, and that made him look even angrier, more forbidding. She didn't understand, though. What did Dermott have to be angry about?

"Yeah, Bridget," he said, his voice sounding husky, the way it sounded after they made love, and yet it wasn't the same. The gentleness was gone. Carrie hadn't been lying, she realized in shock. He'd been serious about ending any relation with her at all, and the knowledge of that sent her emotions reeling. Stunned, she managed to whisper, "Why? What's going on?" Was he that serious about Carrie?

Strangely, her words only increased his anger. She could see it in a chest that rose with labored breath. Raw emotion propelled him forward until they were toe-to-toe. Realizing she'd land in the fire if she backed up farther, she edged to the side, but his hand rose, his fingers curling around the mantel near her head, stopping her. "Look at me, Bridget," he muttered. "What did you expect me to do?"

"What are you talking about?" she managed to say again, her voice raspy with sleep and confusion. For a minute, she wondered if Carrie had called him, reaching him on Ginny's phone downstairs. How else could he have become poisoned against her in only a matter of minutes? "Earlier," she began, her voice shaking, "you were up here…lying beside me, Dermott. We've been in bed all day. How could you—" searching for words, her gaze implored his "—be so angry now? Were you talking to Carrie downstairs?"

"What are you implying?"

"It's like she poisoned you against me!"

"Don't you think that's a little paranoid?" He shot a glance over his shoulder, toward the phone. "What right did you have to answer the call, anyway?"

"Your phone looks like mine," she reminded. "It was dark."

"Earlier you managed to find your own phone."

"You didn't want me to talk to her," she accused. "You were afraid she'd realized…" What must be the truth suddenly hit her. "Did you think you could get away with dating both of us? At the same time? I've known you for years, Dermott. I thought you had more integrity—"

"Dating," he interjected. "Is that what we're doing here?"

"I guess," she muttered, raking a hand through strands of hair that he'd disheveled. "I haven't exactly had time to think about our relationship. Now, have I?"

"You've had a whole lifetime."

"I thought we could—" she paused, searching for the right words "—explore this."

"And then?"

"I don't know." Her eyes searched his as she wondered what he wanted her to say. "We've been friends," she returned, unable to fight the pleading tone creeping into her voice. "Best friends. Don't you…. Didn't you care about that? Apparently, you started sleeping with a woman like Carrie Masterson, and now you're going to walk out on our friendship?"

"A woman like Carrie?"

"I shouldn't have said that," she admitted.

"Carrie's perfect. Interesting. Accomplished—"

"Keep it to yourself," she cut in. "She's not the issue, Dermott. We are."

"Exactly. And so first—" he began, his lips coming so close that in any other circumstance she would have assumed he was going to kiss her.

Her heart fluttered. She hoped he was going to haul her closer, or thrust his fingers into her hair, and say he was sorry. He didn't. "First," he repeated. "You need to understand that I didn't sleep with Carrie Masterson."

She'd never felt so relieved. Silently, she thanked the fates that the image of Carrie wouldn't be hanging over her and Dermott's bed forever. And she *had* been thinking in terms of forever, hadn't she?

"You like that, don't you?" he muttered.

Was this really the same man whose flesh had been joined to hers? Who'd been loving her with such abandon, his hot, hungry mouth trembling on hers, his hands anxious, exploring between her legs, his gentle whispers urging her to come?

"Like *what?*" she managed. "This conversation

doesn't make sense." It was an argument that seemed to exist more in his own mind, as if he'd been having it for years, rather than in the here and now. "You're acting like Dr. Jekyll and Mr. Hyde."

"Oh, so I'*m* the crazy one," he countered, his voice barely audible, sounding rusty in the twilight darkness. "You're the one who dragged me down here because you believe in ghosts. And what about you and all the crazy boyfriends I've helped you run from over the years? Were they really all that crazy, Bridge? Or do you just reject people because you don't want— or can't get—any closer to them? Haven't you ever considered how your own flaws get in the way of your finding love, not some curse?"

"I can't believe you said that," she whispered, feeling the blood drain from her face. "Is this what you think of me?"

He plunged on. "What I meant was that you're pleased as punch, aren't you? You love the fact that I never slept with Carrie Masterson."

She tried to hold her ground. "I'm glad you didn't. Yes."

When his fingers curled more tightly around the wood of the mantel, she shrank back, her emotions even more affected when he said, "I didn't sleep with her, Bridge. Are you happy now? Secure in the fact that I didn't find love?" He shook his head in censure. "What do you want me to do? Pine away for you? Come whenever you need me, and then get lost when you don't?"

"No!"

"I want you to know one thing," he continued. "I

damn well wanted to. I flirted with her. Led her on. Was glad when I came home to find her naked in my apartment. She brought candy, flowers and champagne. For once, I was going to have a proper Valentine's night. And then you had to knock on the door. Do you know why I wanted her most?"

She was afraid to ask. "Why?"

"To get you out of my system," he said, the words coming with such venom that they seemed to carry an expletive behind them, even though none was spoken. "I've chased you for years, and you never cared. Always, it's all about you. Your needs. Your feelings. Your ideas about our relationship."

She'd never been so shocked. "That's not true."

His eyes softened, as if he could admit he'd gone overboard, but then his jaw clenched. Lifting a hand, he stroked a finger down her cheek, his eyes filling with pain as if he anticipated never seeing her again. Instinctively, she reached, her fingers closing tightly around his. Squeezing, she drew his hand to her chest, pressing it to the space of her heart. She watched in stupefaction as he shook his hand free, almost violently.

"Dermott," she whispered, her heart plunging downward, seeming to drop through her own body.

But he simply turned away, headed for the doorway, shoved his feet into his shoes and lifted his duffel from the floor. Then he strode from the room. Feeling paralyzed, she heard him take the stairs downward, two at a time. And then her feet took flight. She ran down the hallway, and from a darkened upstairs window, surrounded by rooms that were probably haunted, she watched him open the door of the SUV.

It slammed shut. A cry escaped her throat as the motor gunned. Then she heard running footsteps. She sank to the floor, just long enough to capture Mug in her arms and draw him against her face, nestling her cheek against his fur. But that couldn't stop the vehicle from starting to move.

No, she couldn't believe this. Had Dermott Brandt really driven out of her life? "And he knows how much I hate to fly," she whispered. Somehow, that seemed like the worst possible thing. Was he really going to leave her stranded? And when he'd always been so wonderfully caring and sweet? Regarding her fears about flying, he'd been so patient, and she'd been patient with him, too.

Just thinking of getting on a plane home, she felt weightless panic engulf her. And where was home now, anyway? She had no ruby slippers to tap together. She loved her folks, but without Dermott, the place where they'd grown up couldn't feel like home again, never in the same way. Damn it, why couldn't she fly? Why was she such a spineless coward? Why hadn't she been able to risk her friendship years ago, so Dermott would be her lover? She'd waited, thinking she'd lose him, but because of her fear, she'd lost him, anyway.

"No," she whispered, unable to believe he was gone. She'd known him all her life. He'd been the person most central to her. He couldn't just disappear. Hadn't he always felt the same as she? That they belonged to each other forever?

"He's gone," she whispered.

It was a very long time before she realized Mug was still in her arms, licking her face, his tiny tongue moving rapidly, trying to keep pace with her tears.

"KEEP DRIVING," Dermott muttered, hunching his shoulders and gripping the wheel. Vaguely, he wondered how many hours he'd been concentrating on the road, pushing out every other thought. Five, maybe six. Some gadget in the SUV had gone buggy. The clock wasn't working, and the defroster was malfunctioning. It had started storming again, and heavy rain was washing over the windshield, the wipers unable to keep pace. He couldn't see anything. Because the windows were fogging, he'd powered them down, which meant cold rain was battering the sleeve of a T-shirt he'd thrown on. High winds came behind it, spreading goose bumps over his skin, but he was too overwrought to feel the chill.

At least the winds got Bridget's scent out of the vehicle. When he'd gotten in, that floral smell had hit him like a wave. She was still everywhere: Her sunglasses were on the dashboard, one of Mug's leashes was beside him on the seat, her baseball cap was looped over the passenger-side visor.

Nevertheless, she was out of his life. He'd done what he'd come here to accomplish.

It would be for the best. This was a fling for her. A passing fancy. They'd been friends, sure. But she'd always rebuffed him. He'd heard how appalled she'd sounded whenever townsfolk assumed they were together, as if she wouldn't have him on a platter.

And she'd really referred to what had happened between them as *dating*. "Dating," he muttered. When he'd asked where she saw them going from here, she'd said she didn't know.

Damn it, his life had been on hold long enough. He wasn't going to take it anymore. She just didn't get it...didn't understand that he'd wasted years fruitlessly wanting her like the world's worst fool. Having her was even worse. His body craved her in a way he'd never anticipated. And he loved her, too. But sometimes love didn't matter. No more than desire. He had to make a life now. For himself.

So he hunched farther over the wheel and kept driving through the dark, stormy night, as if the ghosts of hell were on his heels.

And maybe they were.

BRIDGET STARTLED AWAKE, her head pounding. A hangover. That's what this was. Groaning, she inhaled through clenched teeth as memories flooded back— the fight, Dermott leaving. As her eyes slid to the bedside table, she remembered coming back to the room, crying and drinking more whiskey than she should have.

"Mug," she whispered, but nothing more than the effort of speaking made her head pound harder. Her pup, she realized, was polishing off what was to have been her dinner, hunkering down to better chew at a chicken bone. And then she realized the weather had gone crazy again.

It was freezing in here. Storming. The window was open, she realized as the lace curtains gusted outward. That's why she was so cold! Rising, she ran to shut it, the wind lifting the sundress so it nearly blew over her head. She knew she hadn't opened the window. Dermott couldn't have. A chill raced through her blood and when something metallic slammed against the house, sounding like a falling gutter, she nearly jumped out of her skin.

Wind blew back her hair when she reached the window, and rain soaked her clothes. Grunting, she curled her fingers around the old frame, but it was sticking. With another try, it came down with almost preternatural force, the bottom edge hitting the sill with such force that Bridget was sure the window glass would shatter. She whirled to head for the bed again—only to see Lavinia framed in the doorway. She stopped in her tracks, wondering if she was dreaming.

"We must hurry," urged Lavinia. "I don't have time to chitchat with you tonight. Dark forces are being unleashed in this house."

Yes, Bridget assured herself, even as her feet moved toward Lavinia. *It's just a dream. I know I shut the window.* Still, compelled by a force other than her own volition, she kept following the wavering form into the hallway—and gasped. As Lavinia reached the stairs, a man stepped from the wall. She blinked in the pitch darkness, taking in his rakish grin and the wave of trailing smoke coming from his cigar. "Follow Lavinia," he drawled. "Now, get going, Bridget. If you want your life to work out the way it should, daughter of mine, you'd better do everything she says!"

Her heart beating wildly, she watched the apparition vanish. Had the ghost of her own biological father just spoken to her? There was no time to ponder it. She speeded her steps as the hem of Lavinia's skirt swished around the downstairs banister and was gone. "The curse," Bridget whispered, no longer even caring if this was a dream or reality. Dermott was wrong. The curse really was at the root of their difficulties. What man could have walked away from what she and Dermott had shared? The years they'd supported each other? The gifts they'd given? The hours spent in the blissful pleasure of each others' company?

Granny was right. Until she found that ring, she and her sisters would never find any happiness. She was sure of it. Even now, as she took the stairs two at a time, racing after Lavinia, she couldn't believe Dermott was gone. A hazy feeling came over her when she hit the downstairs landing, just as it had when she'd first seen the ghosts. Vaguely, she felt as if she wasn't even in her own body any longer. She moved forward compulsively, propelled by pure emotion, now reaching for light switches as she passed through downstairs rooms. Even when she flicked them, the rooms remained in darkness, and while she tried to tell herself that was due to a power outage, she knew better. She shivered in terror. It was one thing to be in a haunted house with Dermott, but quite another to be here alone with only Mug.

And with no car. She was in the middle of the woods, surrounded by thickets and swamps. Mavis wasn't entirely friendly, but maybe Bridget should grab Mug and run for the plantation next door. Before she could turn tail, she realized she was in the parlor. As she crossed the threshold, bright light sparked. The wicks of the candles in the chandelier burst into flames, illuminating everything, the walls catching rays of rainbow color. And then the light seemed to spin. Bridget thought her own mind was spinning from drinking too much whisky, and then she thought the chandelier was turning, but now she saw that the light itself was moving.

"Are you going to let that man walk out on you without a fight?" demanded Lavinia, who was standing next to the portrait of Marissa. "Lawdy, you're just standing there looking bedazzled, like a fool."

Bridget started to defend herself, by saying it had been a very long night, but Lavinia continued in a huff, "Now, take that string on the table, or whatever it is, and attach it to Miss Marissa's ring finger."

What was Lavinia talking about? Far beyond worrying over whether ghosts really existed or not, Bridget simply headed for the table. The string turned out to be one of Mug's leashes, a long one with an inbuilt retractor device encased in metal, which made it reroll like a yo-yo. But how was she supposed to attach it to Marissa's finger—and why? Her eyes glanced from Marissa's ring to…

"Oh," she said with a gasp. Her heart stilled, and she felt completely breathless. "Of course," she muttered, everything falling into place. This explained why Forrest had been so adamant about the placement of the painting, not to mention the pose. Only he and Marissa would have understood the secret. Excitedly, Bridget pulled the leash from its holder, pressing a button so it wouldn't retract, then she opened a drawer in the buffet below, found some tape and taped the end of the leash to Marissa's finger.

Slowly, following the exact trajectory of Marissa's pointing finger, which she held up, ostensibly to show off her ring, Bridget crossed the room, stopping only when the leash's other end came to rest on one of the stones of the fireplace, which had been hewn from quarry rock. Her hands roved over the contours, in the exact spot—and caught. Yes…her fingers had curled under one of the jagged rocks, and when she pulled, it slid out effortlessly. The inbuilt drawer was perfectly fitted, and when she peered inside, she was stunned to see its blue velvet lining. There were packets of letters, bound in ribbon, probably exchanged by Forrest and Marissa.

And the ring.

She could only shake her head. Lifting her hand, she began to reach inside the drawer.

And that's when she heard someone drawl, "If I were you, I wouldn't take something that belongs to a ghost."

The cold tone flooded Bridget with horror, and when she whirled, she saw Marissa standing in the doorway, wearing her wedding gown with Mug cradled in her arms. This time, the gown had a spot of blood on the bodice, and her smile did not exactly inspire comfort. "It's taken me years to make contact with the real world," Marissa continued, her voice as icy as the grave. "Years of practice to learn to move objects in rooms. And to lift things, but I couldn't open that drawer yet." She uttered an ugly little laugh.

"Dogs are another matter," she said, "so, here's the plan. You give me my ring for your dog."

Surely, this was just a nightmare! Raw terror uncoiled within Bridget, and she wished she'd never come on this adventure. She'd lost Dermott. Now, she'd endangered Mug! She grabbed the ring, raced forward and quickly dropped it onto the pedestal table, tears filling her eyes. Her heart was beating so fast, she couldn't breathe. "Give me my dog!" she screamed.

Marissa dropped Mug, who raced to Bridget, his dark eyes full of fear, his little legs moving as fast as they could carry him. Squatting, she scooped him into her arms, pressing her face to his and smothering him with kisses. Tears flowed freely. What had she gotten involved in? This was all so crazy! She wanted this nightmare to end! A sob escaped, but as much as she wanted to cover her mouth, she kept her trembling fingers wrapped around the sweet little baby pup she loved so much.

The other woman—or the *thing* that had once been a woman—had paused near the table. Under the portrait, Lavinia was fading, the colors of her dress muting, her outline becoming less defined, as if she was about to disappear because her job here had been done. Feeling Mug burrow into her shoulder, Bridget glanced toward Marissa again, only to realize the other woman was blinking rapidly.

And then the strangest thing happened. The ghost of Miss Marissa Jennings burst into tears. "I'm sorry," she suddenly said, her strained voice barely audible over the crashing storm. "You look so scared. I can see that now. And I really didn't mean to scare any-body. I'm such a terrible…" Her shoulders shaking, she drew a hanky from beneath the lace cuff of her dress and dabbed at her eyes. "I was going to say per-son," she rambled in a honeyed drawl, "but I'm not even a person, am I? Just a silly old ghost, and I've been wretched, punishing everybody in sight. When I saw that fight with you and your beau, I started to feel so guilty."

Her voice trailed off, and then suddenly she began speaking again. "Oh, I suppose I knew my curse had hurt people, but when you came to the house, I finally saw the effect of all my vengeance. Especially when you talked about all your horrid beaus! Antonio and Marco! I just don't know how you survived! At least I'd always had Forrest, who was such a loving, kind, gentle man."

This was just too much. The woman could have hurt Mug, and Dermott was gone. "You're the one who's horrible," Bridget muttered, tears still in eyes that had narrowed to furious slits. "Lavinia and Granny are right. You were spoiled rotten, without a thought for anyone but yourself, Miss Marissa. You can't keep love from other people." And yet, even as she said it, she realized that was exactly what Der-mott had accused her of doing. Her heart wrenched and she gasped, holding back a sob of her own.

"I know," whispered Marissa. "Could you please forgive me?"

Bridget wasn't in a forgiving mood, so she was still considering when things took a twist so unex-pected that Bridget became even more convinced none of this was happening. Yes, this just had to be a dream. She watched as Forrest Hartley swept into the room, wearing his Confederate uniform, a sword strapped to his side. Bending on one knee in front of Marissa, he gathered her hand in his. "I've waited years to hear those words, my darling," he drawled in a low, sexy baritone voice that made Bridget's knees weak, despite the circumstances of her own romantic life, and the fact that he was a ghost. "All these years, I've waited," he explained. "Held captive, not by the Yankees, my darling love, but by the powers that be."

"The powers that be?" Marissa murmured as he reached for the pedestal table, lifted the ring with ease and brought it to Marissa's finger.

"As long as you had such vengeance in your heart, love was no longer known to you, my dear. But now that you see the error of your ways, I was able to follow your voice through the rooms of our home and find you again. Years," he repeated. "So many wasted years. Will you be with me now, my darling, beautiful bride? For all eternity?"

"Yes," Marissa whispered. "Yes."

And then, as Bridget watched in astonishment, the ghost of Forrest Hartley slid the ring onto Miss Marissa's finger. The second it came to rest comfortably, both vanished, as if in a puff of smoke. One second, they were there. The next, they were gone. Bridget wrenched her head toward Marissa's portrait, but Lavinia was gone now, too. Had she been sleepwalking? Had she just awakened? Would she run upstairs to find this was all a horrible nightmare, and Dermott was still here?

But no. It had happened, hadn't it? The smell of burning cigars had vanished. Suddenly, a gust swept the room, blowing out the candles that had lighted the chandelier. And Bridget was left in darkness.

Her feet took flight then, and she ran through the empty, dark house, hoping she really wasn't alone, after all. Surely, since she'd found the ring, the curse had ended. And that would mean Dermott would still be sleeping in the bed. Gasping, she reached the threshold of the bedroom.

But Dermott was gone.

10

WHEN HIS PHONE RANG—he'd reprogrammed the ringer to "Bolero"—Dermott quickly unbuttoned his sport coat, then glanced to where the instrument attached to his belt. His lips parted as he stared at the number, his chest constricting. Bridget, he thought. Again. She'd been calling ever since he'd left Florida, but he wasn't going to call her back. No way. His trip to L.A. had helped him block memories of their time together. The director had turned out to be demanding, which meant long nights in the studio. Only when he'd returned to New York had he found himself with too much time on his hands. Fortunately, after Allison and Kenneth's wedding, he was going back to L.A. for another few days.

When he glanced up, Carrie was studying him. She looked gorgeous, too. Her dark hair was drawn up into a fancy knot, and tiny white flowers were nestled in the strands. She was wearing the kind of little black dress she favored, with spaghetti straps and a low-dipping neckline that showcased the slope of her breasts. Slowly, she swirled a goblet of burgundy that matched the wine color of her lips. Everything in her eyes said she knew it had been Bridget. He schooled his features into a mask, as if nothing had occurred and glanced over the dinner table, which had just been cleared. "Would you like to see the dessert menu? They have amazing pastries."

She didn't answer immediately. Shortly after he'd returned, he'd asked her out for dinner, and she'd put him off until tonight. Now he wished he hadn't picked this eatery on Greenwich Street. It was perfect for a private rendezvous: quiet, discreet and not on any tourist maps. It also happened to be in the neighborhood where he and Bridget had grown up, and they'd eaten here countless times.

Carrie had continued swirling the wine in her glass. Now, her eyes met his over the candlelight. "Hmm. So, you told her."

He nodded. "I'm ready to move on with my life."

It was the wrong time for "Bolero" to blare again. He uttered a soft sound of frustration. "I'm sorry. I should have turned the phone off." It wasn't Bridget this time, though. When he glanced down, he saw it was her sister, Edie, no doubt calling to ask once more if he could offer some input on the music selections for the Darden wedding.

"You say you should have turned it off…" Carrie's voice was low. "Then why didn't you, Dermott?" Before he could respond, she began to rise, saying, "Will you excuse me for a moment?"

"Sure." He rose as she did, setting his napkin on the table, reseating himself only when she was gone. Sighing, he glided a hand through his hair, his eyes landing on the lit fire in the hearth. That, too, just reminded him of making love to Bridget in the firelight at her grandmother's. Abruptly, he shifted his gaze. Outside, through lace-covered windows, snow was swirling, the streets already looking slick. Allison and Kenneth, he realized, were going to have a white wedding tomorrow morning. And then he startled. "What the…"

Quickly rising to his feet, he headed for the front of the restaurant, not stopping until he reached the door. The maître d' had been standing behind a podium surveying the guest book, and now he circled it, straightening the tie under his black jacket as he came to stand beside Dermott. Lightly, he touched his sleeve, and in a low murmur, said, "Sir, she asked me to tell you…"

Dermott's eyes had settled on Carrie, who'd retrieved her wrap from the coat-check room. She was standing in the windswept road, under a street lamp, with her arm raised. A cab came into view, and when it stopped, she opened the door and got inside without a backward glance. Dermott returned his eyes to the other man's. "Yes?"

The maître d' paused. "She asked me to inform you that you're in love with another woman."

He supposed he was. Lifting his fingers, Dermott touched the window glass, watching as the cab pulled away. That was the thing about Carrie, he thought. Not only was she bright, smart and accomplished. She also had an incredible amount of class.

"Too bad love's sometimes not enough," he whispered.

"I CAN'T DO THIS," Bridget managed to say as her mother, sisters and granny circled around her, read-justing her bridesmaid's gown as if Bridget were merely a doll they were dressing. "I don't want to see Dermott at all right now, much less…"

During a wedding. But she would. She'd never do anything to mar Allison and Kenneth's perfect day. When she'd seen Carrie, who'd come in to look over the gowns, she and the other woman had acted as if absolutely nothing had happened. And Bridget intended to continue doing so.

"Don't worry," Edie cooed. "You and Dermott will make up. You always do."

"This is different, Edie."

Her mother sent her a startled glance. "Oh, Bridge," she murmured. "Different? How? You've known him for years. You two are such good friends."

And more, Bridget wanted to say. That was what was different. But this was her business. Her life. And this really was Allison's special day. Besides, Dermott was right. She'd taken him for granted and held him back. Probably a lot of wonderful women could have already given him a lovely home and children. Not to mention countless nights of spicy sex and physical love. Carrie's words had cut her to the quick. So had Dermott's.

Mostly because they were true. She'd been so self-ish, just like Miss Marissa, expecting him to be her best friend when he needed so much more. It had taken their words a while to sink in, but Bridget wouldn't hurt Dermott anymore. She was going to be brave. Her chin suddenly quivered, but she clamped her jaw tight. Yes…she was going to walk down an aisle wearing pink with Dermott Brandt, and she was going to stay calm while she listened to the vows, even though she always cried at weddings, anyway. But she was going to leave the church with him, and she wasn't going to shed one tear. Or at least not until they reached the front doors.

But why did it have to be Saint Paul's? she suddenly thought, her heart wrenching. This was her favorite church, the oldest in Manhattan, and the one in which George Washington's pew was still displayed, roped off by velvet. The interior was pink-and-blue, and the ceiling was hung with original chandeliers, all of which were nearly as beautiful as the one in Ginny's parlor. "This wedding's hopelessly romantic," Bridget suddenly murmured. "Oh, Edie, you did such a great job for Allison and Kenneth."

"I know this is hard, Bridget," her sister returned, looking stunning in her own suit. "I'm sure whatever's happening with you and Dermott isn't as serious as you think. You know how emotional you are at weddings. You can pull this off. Just act like you're not fighting with him. And don't forget that I really need your help."

"No problem." She paused. "Is Allison okay?"

"Calmer than you are," remarked Viv worriedly. "And as soon as the wedding's over, I want to talk to you about whatever's going on with you and Dermott."

Marley had already left the dressing rooms, to be

seated with Cash, who was her date. Bridget's eyes slid to Granny Ginny, who looked adorable in a navy-and-white plaid suit with matching two-tone shoes. "I'm glad you decided to stay in town for a few more days, Granny," Bridget murmured.

So much had happened while she'd been gone. Marley and Cash had gotten really close, so much so that Bridget wondered if they intended to announce an engagement, curse or no curse. And although Edie's whole world had been rocked by the fact that the reality show *Rate the Dates* had discussed the Hartley curse on national television, harming her wedding business by costing her clients, she was keeping a clear head. Truly, she couldn't have done a better job. Everything was perfect for Allison and Kenneth—the flowers, the music, the gowns.

Bridget wasn't about to ruin it. For the next hour, she vowed, she'd refuse to think. She was going to smile. And she was going to walk down that aisle perfectly, so as not to mar the pictures Allison and Kenneth would have forever. She'd look at Dermott just as she had at Carrie. As if nothing had happened. Her hands tightened around the stems of a bouquet. The flowers weren't as fuzzy as Mug, of course, but they were something to hold on to.

"Showtime," said Edie brightly. "Now, we've got to get out of here. Get you two seated. Pop's already in a pew next to Marley and Cash. So, Granny and Mom, I want to make sure you're all together."

"You look gorgeous," Viv said to Bridget. "A real

addition to the party. I can't wait to see you standing there next to Allison."

And Bridget couldn't wait to see Allison. She was in the next room, alone with her mother. Bridget hoped with all her heart that this marriage would be perfect for her friends. She felt somebody grab her arm, and when she glanced away from her mother who was heading for the door now, she realized her granny was trying to get her attention. "Yes, Granny?"

Her elderly relative's voice cracked. "I'm so sorry, baby," she drawled. A papery hand touched Bridget's cheek. "It's the curse." Sighing, she shook her head. "You're in love with Dermott. I can see it as plain as day, even though your mother and sisters are so used to thinking of you as best friends that they haven't even guessed. You found the ring," she added. "So I just don't understand it. I was so sure that would lift the curse." With that, Granny turned on her heel and headed for the door, with Viv and Edie close on her heels, glancing back to say, "You do look beautiful, dear."

Bridget sighed. She didn't understand why the curse hadn't lifted, either. Her last night in Granny Ginny's house was a blur. Overwrought by the fight with Dermott, she knew she'd drunk a bit much. She rarely did, if ever. But the whiskey had tasted so good, burning down her throat. And then she'd had that terrible dream. If it was a dream. The last thing she remembered, she'd been in the parlor, and all the lights had gone out. The next day, when she'd awakened, the whiskey bottle beside the bed was gone, as surely as if Jasper had taken it. Dermott hadn't returned.

And the ring had been sitting where the whisky bottle had been. Whatever the case, Granny was right. Finding the ring hadn't mattered. She'd raced back to New York, barely caring that she was flying and she'd tried to call Dermott. But he'd never answered, nor had he called her back.

And now she was about to see him for the first time.

It WAS WORSE than Dermott had anticipated. Bridget looked so damn beautiful. She was all dressed in pink. Her hair was covered by a dainty white cap, and the dress was almost a replica of that worn by Allison, although the skirt wasn't as full. The flowers she carried were white, too. And every time he looked at her, he had to fight the urge to turn around, and simply stride down the aisle into the harsh winter air, if only to get away from her scent. February in Florida had been cold. New York had turned brutal. Surely, the air outside would clear his head.

Not that the ceremony would be affected by the weather. The roads were clear and the limos ready to take everyone to the Brooklyn Botanical Garden for a reception. He just wished it would all end soon. He'd exchanged words with Carrie, briefly, but really, there wasn't much to be said. She was right. He was in love with Bridget, but he had no idea what to do about it. What? Start dating? as Bridget had suggested.

It was insulting. She'd been his lifeblood for years,

and he couldn't give any more of his heart to a woman who didn't feel the same for him. She'd greeted him so coolly, too. As if she completely accepted how he'd left her stranded. The eyes that met his, when he'd crooked his arm, ready to walk her down the aisle, had been steady, just like the hand that had slid over his arm, making him burst inside with unrequited need. Countless times since he'd last seen her, he'd imagined her naked in his arms again.

Pushing aside the thoughts, he tried to concentrate on the vows, but that was worse. Allison and Kenneth had written them, and the trajectory of their romance had been so much like his and Bridget's. Friends to lovers. Except that Allison and Kenneth were tying the knot.

"I thought you were just a friend," Allison was saying. "For years, you were in my life. We did everything together, never knowing we were building the foundation for the eternity we're about to share..."

Kenneth picked up the thread. "All the years we went to school together, ate lunch in the same place, and saw each other on weekends, I never even imagined it would be this face..." As Kenneth's voice trailed off, he lifted his hand to Allison's cheek. "This face I'd look into forever...."

It was too much. It was as if Allison and Kenneth had written their own vows with Dermott and Bridget in mind, although they'd done no such thing. Dermott wasn't proud of it, but he blocked out the rest. Silently, he counted to ten, wishing Carrie's eyes weren't on his

back, and wishing even more that Bridget's arm
hadn't curled so easily around his arm earlier, and that
she wasn't standing only a few feet away now.

Relief flooded him during the kiss. More when
the organ sounded. He was only minutes from free-
dom. Everything seemed to happen in slow motion.
The bride and groom headed out. He turned. Bridget turned. She slid her hand over his arm once more,
and somehow, smiling as if neither of them had a care
in the world, they traversed the white aisle once
more, not pausing until they reached the front doors
of Saint Paul's.

And then the funniest thing happened. Bridget
turned away, but not before he caught her glimpse of
horror and panic. Her blue eyes, so steady before,
were shimmering with tears. Abruptly, realizing he'd
seen them, she simply pushed through the doors and
ran onto Fifth Avenue. She was nowhere near as unaffected by what had happened as he had assumed.
"Of course, she isn't," he murmured.

And then he ran after her.

SHE'D BLOWN IT. She'd meant to be brave. She wasn't
going to cry. But he'd caught her! The bracing wind
outside came as a relief. It stung her skin, giving her
something to concentrate on rather than Dermott.
Aware she was creating a spectacle on the sidewalk,
she turned a corner and ran blindly down the side
street, having no idea where she was going, her
pumps slick on the snow, her hands clenched against
the wind. She lifted her skirts, hoping to move faster.

She had to get away from the church, from the romance of the wedding and Dermott.

Suddenly, she gasped, realizing her feet had taken her toward his apartment. Of course she'd run there! The place was like a homing device for her. Was there no escape? Feeling air knife into her lungs, she ran across Church Street, not stopping until her fingers were twined through the gaps in a chain-link fence. She glanced up, and another wave of sorrow hit her. She'd run right into what the country was now calling Ground Zero.

There was nothing "zero" about it! she thought. Her whole life was here. There was a big, gaping hole in the ground, just like there was a big, gaping hole in her life right now, and as she stared at it, nothing made sense. So many times, she'd come here and said a prayer for those who'd died. Like everyone, she'd been deeply touched by the pain of those who'd lost loved ones. Shuddering against her tears and the cold, she looked past where the stately, proud towers had stood to Dermott's building, which rose into a winter sky as if from dust. She loved that building, too. Was she never going inside it again? Never going to grin at his doorman as she dropped off some trinket she'd bought for him?

Hands closed over her shoulders, and she spun around. When she saw it was Dermott, she tried to mask her pain, but she couldn't. Shifting the bouquet from one hand to another, she swiped at her face. "Weddings," she murmured. "They always make me cry."

"I don't believe that's what's bothering you, Bridge."

She tried to make light, even though she was starting to shiver. It really was cold out here, hovering near zero. And he looked unbelievably handsome in the gorgeous tux. Because it was an all-white wedding, she looked like a bride at the moment, too. "I'm fine. I promise. I just need to be by myself. Why don't you go inside?" To Carrie.

He read her mind. "We're not together."

She couldn't help but ask, "You're not?"

"Of course we're not," he muttered, his hands circling her waist. He angled his head down so his lips nearly brushed hers.

She wanted to turn away, but she sank into his arms, the warmth of his embrace feeling so perfect. For days, she'd craved his touch. How could he have left her in bed? Left their love nest, where he'd made her his? Reaching, he caught her free hand and drew it against his heart, then he leaned and kissed her. Their lips caught in the wind, their tongues feeling cold, but warming as they touched. By the time he was through plundering her mouth, her tears were falling freely. Overwhelmed, she wrenched and stared into the gaping hole in the ground. She could see workmen deep in the pit, looking so far away that they could have been a child's plastic toys.

"I can't remember what they look like," she found herself saying, glancing quickly over her shoulder. "Remember when we used to say they destroyed our view of the rest of Manhattan?" She didn't have to explain that she was speaking of the towers. When he nodded, she shook her head. "I wish we'd never said that."

"Bridge," he said softly, his hand on her shoulder once more, willing her to turn to face him again.

Instead, she said, "I used to come here, just to try to remember them, after I left your apartment. I'd will myself to remember. But we've lived here all our lives. We saw those buildings since we were kids." Suddenly, she sobbed. "What if the Chrysler Building was gone tomorrow? The Empire State? Grand Central?" Now she was crying so hard she could barely talk. "Would we remember any of them? What if I never saw you again?"

He kissed her again, more thoroughly this time, his lips moving slowly on hers, feeding them with warmth. "It's not going to happen," he said huskily.

"I'm sorry I took you for granted," she managed to whisper, turning in his arms, trying to explain. "I thought you'd always be here. I never even questioned it. I thought you'd always be mine. I thought if I gave more, that…"

"You'd lose me?"

She nodded solemnly. "Absolutely. And I could never do that, Derm. Never. I can't live without you. Please don't leave me. Please promise me. Please, I'm begging you. Please—"

"You're running from me, remember?"

"Not anymore."

It was all the confession of love he needed. Lifting the hand curled on his chest, he studied the ring. Then his eyes narrowed. "It doesn't look the same. It looks…"

Brighter. Shinier. More like real diamonds. One day she'd tell him the whole story, but now she settled for saying, "It's not. I found the real ring after you left, and this is it." Her voice hitched. "Granny said I should have it, since I'm the one who found it. I want to wear it forever." She smiled through her tears. "The Hartley engagement ring," she whispered. "It has so much history, so much significance. It was lost for so long, and the adventure of finding it is how we became lovers." She gulped in air. "And…"

"It's on the wrong finger," Dermott finished.

Her breath caught. "Yes. I suppose it is. I hadn't really thought of it that way."

A second later, Dermott was on his knees in the snow, bending just as Forrest Hartley had done days before. Unless, of course, that had been an illusion. A mere figment of Bridget's overactive imagination. Carefully, she twisted the ring on her right hand, gave it to Dermott, then extended her left.

As he slipped the ring back on her finger—the right finger—he said, "Will you marry me, Bridget Benning?"

As the ring come to rest where it was to remain for the rest of her life, she felt a strange peace descend, and suddenly, she was sure that finding it really had put the ghosts of Hartley House to rest. When Granny Ginny returned, Bridget could almost guarantee she wouldn't hear a peep out of those wily souls for a good long while. "Yes," she whispered. "Oh, yes."

Dermott rose, a sudden, radiant smile claiming

his lips as he circled his arms around her waist once more. Swiftly, he settled that smile right on top of hers. As he sealed their union with the kiss, heat surged between them that was no match for the frigid winter air blowing through their clothes. Soon, she was shivering in his arms, less from the cold than the sensual warmth he generated.

"We'd better go in before they miss us," she whispered against his lips.

"Yeah," he said simply, casting a quick glance toward his apartment, as if he'd like nothing more than to take her there and ravish her.

When his arm stretched around her shoulders, she suddenly realized she was home for good. She'd always live here, in this city. And with this man. Turning just for a second, she glanced over her shoulder, and in that time—a space that could have been a heartbeat or the snap of a finger—she saw them. Two shining silver towers rising in smoke and haze, floating in the air, looking exactly like the images she'd always seen of lost cities. Such as Brigadoon. Or Atlantis.

And then she turned again to look into Dermott Brandt's dark, magical eyes. He was simply smiling back, and with so much love and heat that she knew something truly mysterious had happened to them. "I guess lost things are always found," she whispered to him, stretching on her tiptoes to kiss him as she nestled in his embrace. "Even our love."

Angling farther down, to better drink in her mouth, he corrected, feathering his lips over hers and saying,

"Especially our love, Bridge. It's real." Like memory, itself, or the indelible traces left by all the things that had gone before them, love like this had to endure.

* * * * *

In May, look for I THEE BED…,
the third romance in the
BIG APPLE BRIDES *miniseries.*

Supposedly, Bridget's finding the lost Hartley diamond ended the wedding curse that's haunted all the Bennings' love lives. Edie's not so sure. Ever since the curse was announced on national television, dates have been far and few between. And even worse, her clients are jumping ship. She's the walking cliché—a wedding planner who can't get hitched.

Can her new assistant at Big Apple Brides help her set things right, or does the sexy guy have his own agenda?

HARLEQUIN

Temptation

It's hot...and out of control!

Don't miss these bold and ultrasexy books!

BUILDING A BAD BOY by Colleen Collins
Harlequin Temptation #1016
March 2005

WARM & WILLING by Kate Hoffmann
Harlequin Temptation #1017
April 2005

HER LAST TEMPTATION by Leslie Kelly
Harlequin Temptation #1028
June 2005

Look for these books at your favorite retail outlet.

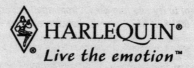

HARLEQUIN®
Live the emotion™

www.eHarlequin.com   HTHEAT

If you enjoyed what you just read,
then we've got an offer you can't resist!

Take 2 bestselling
love stories FREE!

Plus get a FREE surprise gift!

Clip this page and mail it to Harlequin Reader Service®

IN U.S.A.
3010 Walden Ave.
P.O. Box 1867
Buffalo, N.Y. 14240-1867

IN CANADA
P.O. Box 609
Fort Erie, Ontario
L2A 5X3

YES! Please send me 2 free Blaze™ novels and my free surprise gift. After receiving them, if I don't wish to receive anymore, I can return the shipping statement marked cancel. If I don't cancel, I will receive 4 brand-new novels each month, before they're available in stores! In the U.S.A., bill me at the bargain price of $3.99 plus 25¢ shipping and handling per book and applicable sales tax, if any*. In Canada, bill me at the bargain price of $4.47 plus 25¢ shipping and handling per book and applicable taxes**. That's the complete price and a savings of at least 10% off the cover prices—what a great deal! I understand that accepting the 2 free books and gift places me under no obligation ever to buy any books. I can always return a shipment and cancel at any time. Even if I never buy another book from Harlequin, the 2 free books and gift are mine to keep forever.

150 HDN DZ9K
350 HDN DZ9L

Name	(PLEASE PRINT)
Address	Apt.#
City	State/Prov. Zip/Postal Code

Not valid to current Harlequin Blaze™ subscribers.

Want to try two free books from another series?
Call 1-800-873-8635 or visit www.morefreebooks.com.

* Terms and prices subject to change without notice. Sales tax applicable in N.Y.
** Canadian residents will be charged applicable provincial taxes and GST.
   All orders subject to approval. Offer limited to one per household.
® and ™ are registered trademarks owned and used by the trademark owner or its licensee.

BLZ04R   ©2004 Harlequin Enterprises Limited.

eHARLEQUIN.com

The Ultimate Destination for Women's Fiction

The ultimate destination for women's fiction.
Visit eHarlequin.com today!

GREAT BOOKS:
- We've got something for everyone—and at great low prices!
- Choose from new releases, backlist favorites, Themed Collections and preview upcoming books, too.
- Favorite authors: Debbie Macomber, Diana Palmer, Susan Wiggs and more!

EASY SHOPPING:
- Choose our convenient "bill me" option. No credit card required!
- Easy, secure, 24-hour shopping from the comfort of your own home.
- Sign-up for free membership and get $4 off your first purchase.
- Exclusive online offers: FREE books, bargain outlet savings, hot deals.

EXCLUSIVE FEATURES:
- Try Book Matcher—finding your favorite read has never been easier!
- Save & redeem Bonus Bucks.
- Another reason to love Fridays— Free Book Fridays!

Shop online
at www.eHarlequin.com today!

INTBB204

HARLEQUIN®

Temptation

One frantic bride, one missing groom
and twenty-four hours for three
couples to discover they're meant
to live happily ever after....

24 Hours: The Wedding

Don't miss these fabulous stories by three of
Temptation's favorite authors!

FALLING FOR YOU by Heather MacAllister
Harlequin Temptation #1014
March 2005

KISS AND RUN by Barbara Daly
Harlequin Temptation #1018
April 2005

ONE NIGHT IN TEXAS by Jane Sullivan
Harlequin Temptation #1022
May 2005

On sale this spring at your favorite retail outlet.

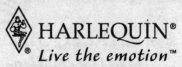

HARLEQUIN®
Live the emotion™

www.eHarlequin.com   HT24W

HARLEQUIN®
Temptation

AMERICAN HEROES

These men are heroes—
strong, fearless...
And impossible to resist!

Join bestselling authors Lori Foster, Donna Kauffman
and Jill Shalvis as they deliver up

MEN OF COURAGE

Harlequin anthology
May 2003

Followed by *American Heroes* miniseries
in Harlequin Temptation

RILEY by Lori Foster
June 2003

SEAN by Donna Kauffman
July 2003

LUKE by Jill Shalvis
August 2003

Don't miss this sexy new miniseries by some of
Temptation's hottest authors!

Available at your favorite retail outlet.

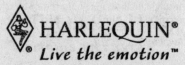

HARLEQUIN®
Live the emotion™

Visit us at www.eHarlequin.com

HTAH

Silhouette® *Desire*®

presents:

**New York Times
bestselling author**

JOAN HOHL

A MAN APART

(SD #1640, available
March 2005)

The moment rancher Justin Grainger laid eyes on
sexy Hannah Deturk, he vowed not to leave town
without getting into her bed. Their whirlwind affair left
them both wanting more. But Hannah feared falling
for a loner like Justin could only mean heartache...
unless she convinced him to be a man apart no longer.

Available at your favorite retail outlet.

Visit Silhouette Books at www.eHarlequin.com

SDAMA0205

Blaze™

◈ HARLEQUIN® *Blaze*™

When three women go to a lock-and-key
party to meet sexy singles, they never
expect to find their perfect matches....

#166 HARD TO HANDLE
by Jamie Denton
January 2005

#170 ON THE LOOSE
by Shannon Hollis
February 2005

#174 SLOW RIDE
by Carrie Alexander
March 2005

Indulge in these three blazing hot stories today!

Lock & Key
Unlock the possibilities...

On sale at your favorite retail outlet.

HBLK04